I0567922

Second-year university student Edie Whitecrow gobbles up each course on Indigenous studies. If only she could experience the lives of her *Anishinaabe* ancestors instead of reading about them. On her way to a Halloween party decked out as a historical Ojibway maiden, she spies a corn maze in a spot known to be barren.

A scarecrow figure beckons Edie to enter with the enticing offer of making her biggest wish come true. She jumps at the chance and finds herself in the past, face to face with the man who haunts her dreams — the handsome brave Thunder Bear. He claims he's spent twelve years waiting for Gitche Manidoo to send her to him.

Life in the eighteenth century isn't what Edie romanticized about, though. When her conscience is tested, she must choose between the modern day or the world of her descendants — where the man she was born for resides.

The unauthorized reproduction or distribution of this copyrighted work is illegal. Criminal copyright infringement, including infringement without monetary gain, is investigated by the FBI and is punishable by up to 5 years in federal prison and a fine of $250,000.

This book is a work of fiction. Names, characters, places, and incidents either are products of the author's imagination or are used fictitiously. Any resemblance to actual events or locales or persons, living or dead, is entirely coincidental.

Born for This
Copyright © 2021 Maggie Blackbird
ISBN: 978-1-4874-3448-9
Cover art by Martine Jardin

All rights reserved. Except for use in any review, the reproduction or utilization of this work in whole or in part in any form by any electronic, mechanical or other means, now known or hereafter invented, is forbidden without the written permission of the publisher.

Published by eXtasy Books Inc

Look for us online at:
www.eXtasybooks.com

Born for This Maizemerized

By

Maggie Blackbird

DEDICATION

In memory of my grandmothers, two strong Anishinaabe-Kweg I truly admire.

Thank you to my husband and the Mals for your love and support.

Thank you to D.S. Dehel for your feedback. You da best.

Thank you to my father for the information and help with the research.

Thank you to my editor, Emmy, my proofer, Bri, cover artist, Martin Jardine, and EIC Jay. As always, I couldn't have done this without your help.

CHAPTER ONE: HOLLOW MAN

When Grandmother Moon was full, Ojibway women honored Her through an elaborate or simple ceremony, asking the great lady who governed the water and the female cycle for guidance and new energy—what Edie had done with Koko before she'd left for the Halloween party this evening.

The luminescent orb had shone in the windshield from Edie's home reserve to Highway Six-Twenty-One. Maybe Grandmother Moon was trying to say something, because She was a constant presence on the drive.

Edie cranked the car stereo. The music blasted through the speakers. There was something mystical, even spooky about The Cult, an older rock group Mom still listened to. Just as the moon seemed to speak to Edie, so did the music with its magical guitar and the singer's baritone wail, the reason why she'd ripped all of the band's CDs into digital format.

Straight and odd long curves saturated the highway leading to the Indian Reserve where the Halloween party was taking place. Right now, she was on the straight stretch. The dips in the road were as gentle as being rocked in a cradleboard, or moss bag, as Koko liked to call a *tiginaaganan*.

Edie's friends had urged her to attend the party. They'd exclaimed she had to meet the most fab guy ever produced by the First Nations communities, so she'd made the jaunt from Winnipeg for the weekend.

As for her trip, it wasn't about meeting a new guy. It was about having another chance to don what her female Ojibway ancestors once wore.

She couldn't resist rubbing the doeskin material of the dress Koko had sewn for the occasion with matching moccasins. The fringes on the skirt were like tickling feathers brushing Edie's calves.

Each time she drove from Manitoba into Ontario, the steep hills, massive rock cuts, and endless lakes of the northwest were welcoming open arms, as if a whistling wind breezing through the trees was bidding her hello to a special place where she belonged, instead of on the prairies where she attended university.

Plus, the drive from school was only three and a half hours from the Rainy River area where she'd grown up.

Tonight, all was still. Even quiet.

One headlight, probably from a motorcycle, appeared behind her. The weather was unusually warm for the end of October, but driving a bike at this time of the year was rather brave.

Edie adjusted her rearview mirror to block out the light, although the driver used his low beam. She also slowed to let him safely pass. Maybe he was a partygoer, making his way to the Halloween bash. Or he could've crossed the international bridge in Rainy River, an American coming from Baudette. Or he could be a Canadian approaching from the town of Fort Frances.

The engine of the bike didn't possess the distinct sound of a Harley Davidson, nor did the sporting and athletic roar resemble the high squeal of the Asian-made racing machines. Whatever he drove was loud enough to cut into her music.

He was by her side. She stole a quick peek out the side window at a helmeted silhouette of black.

He also turned his head.

Déjà vu was a hidden being lurking in the backseat, its claws settling on Edie's shoulders. For a moment, her heart stood still. The haunting dream since she was but a child unfurled through her brain—a strong hand possessing long fingers stretching to reach hers, and a man's black, narrow eyes staring through the mist.

Edie swatted the air, shooing away the crazy thought. The guy on the motorcycle was simply passing her on the highway. But his continuous attention opened up a discomforting twitch at the back of her neck.

With a tilt of his helmet, he whizzed past her. The bike slid from the left lane and into the right. He was moving so fast that his taillight quickly vanished into the night. The man had better slow down. In the fall, deer tended to pop up out of nowhere.

Edie sank further in her seat and tapped her nail on the steering wheel. He couldn't be a partygoer. From what she'd spied, there'd been no costume draping his masculine silhouette. Or maybe he was the man hidden in the mist, stretching his hand to hers, giving her a glimpse of his long nose, thin lips, and razor-cutting cheekbones.

Get real. If Mom snuck into your thoughts, for the bazillionth time she'd tell you to get out of your imagination and quit thinking about the old days.

She bounced her left foot in beat to the song. Maybe Mom was right. Edie's obsession with their ancestors must stop. Fat chance of that happening, because her BA major was Indigenous Studies. Plus, what was wrong about wishing for a life amongst her relations from long ago?

The corner of her eye caught the moonlight shining down on a . . . corn maze.

Huh?

The land to her right, as far as she knew, was barren. A simple field. She turned her head and lowered the volume on the stereo. For goodness sake, she *was* staring at a corn maze. How amazing. *Mandaamin* was sacred to her people and what they served for the fall feast held every late September.

She'd never seen an actual maze before. Farmers didn't go out of their way to create elaborate labyrinths in the Rainy River Valley. Instead, they planted in straight rows.

She had to check this out.

Edie pulled over. Much to her delight, she didn't have to park on the side of the road, because grass trampled into black velvet earth led down to the maze. She guided her car along the smooth surface.

How could this have happened? She squinted. Even weirder, the brown husks were dead.

A scarecrow stood sentry at the entrance.

Her phone blipped. She swiped the cell from her purse and checked the text message.

Where are you? The party's already started.

The message was from Tamara, naturally. Her best friend wanted to set Edie up with the mystery guest who was supposed to show at the party. Not that again.

I'm checking something out. Give me twenty minutes.

The maze must be a mirage of some sort. Nobody would create something like this without everyone in the Rainy River District knowing about it and coming to peek at the elaborate construction.

Hurry. I told you. He's smokin'. Freaking f-ing hot. He comes from a rez in Manitoba. He goes to U of M. He's in his second year for his master's in political science. I'm only gonna be able to hold off the girls for so long.

Edie sighed and typed.

You told me all this already. I'll be there soon.

You can't keep your legs closed forevah, gf!

Gosh, what was the big deal of her nonexistent sex life? She couldn't be blamed for staying a virgin. The right guy had never come along. Maybe because, as Mom said, *Stop with the fantasies of the perfect boy. Just because there're no warriors in this day doesn't mean boys in university can't be heroic in their own way. For once, please put away your books and go out and live.*

But those books on her ancestors were Edie's most trusted companions.

Okay, give me a second to do this. Then I'll be right there.

Do what?????

You'd never believe me.

Edie shucked aside the phone. She shut off her car and got out. A hint of a breeze ruffled the fringes on the bottom of her doeskin dress. There hadn't been a smidgen of wind earlier, even all day, so why now?

The breeze seemed to push on her backside in the direction of the scarecrow, as if *Animkiig,* the Thunderbirds, were guiding her forward. Impossible. There was no storm. Not one cloud lazily floated in the midnight-blue sky.

Movement came from the scarecrow. Its hanging head creaked in her direction.

A shock of fright gripped Edie by the spine. She tried to halt, but the breeze continued to nudge her forward, as if reassuring her there was nothing to fear.

She shuffled her moccasin-wrapped feet forward. The alarm didn't dissipate. She bit down on her index finger, nibbling at the skin so she wouldn't bite the long nails she'd had manicured for the party.

The scarecrow raised its hand and curled one bony finger at her.

Ghastly. From what she could see, there wasn't any muscle on the being, only bone and flesh. The tattered clothing hung on the creature that lacked anything firm beneath to fill out the material of flannel and denim. The shredded shirt and pants covered the scarecrow from head to toe. Even the straw hat hid its face.

Edie slapped her hand to her mouth. Could this be *Mandaamin*, the corn spirit of the *Anishinaabeg* who'd sacrificed himself centuries ago to feed the People? Of course. Who else could summon a maze from nowhere? Who else could call the Thunderbirds to coax her forward, even when terror racked her body?

Suddenly, the grip of dread holding her spine vanished.

The scarecrow kept curling its finger.

"*Mandaamin*, is it you?" she called out.

The long-sleeved plaid shirt and jeans ruffled in the slight breeze. The scarecrow pointed at what was the entrance to the maze.

Edie cast a sidelong glance at the dead corn stalks and back to the hideous being. "*Mandaamin*, is it you?"

The only reply was the whistling of the wind.

She edged in closer, tilting her head slightly and still squinting. "*Mandaamin*, is it you?"

"Whatever you wish for . . . your wish will come true." The scarecrow's voice was the deep echo found in a canyon.

Shaking, Edie planted one foot behind her. The breeze wrapped her, again pushing her forward. Her heart seemed to slide from her chest and into her parched throat. She licked her dry lips. "Wh-who are you?"

"Whatever you wish for . . . your wish will come true." For the second time, the scarecrow pointed at the opening to the maze.

Edie drew back her shoulders and jutted out her chin. "Who are you?"

"Does it matter?" With the slow movement of a swooping feather, the creature extended his arm and again motioned his hand at the entrance. "You will find the path to what you desire. Take caution, though, for once you are there, if you decide to return, you can never go back."

"Wait. I have questions."

The life within the scarecrow deflated, as if someone had plucked open its cap. She could almost hear the hiss of energy draining from the being. The baggy shirt and oversized pants melted against its skin of bones.

Edie stepped in closer. She set her hand on the scarecrow's arm and shook him. Nothing, other than the jingling of his lifeless body.

"*Mandaamin*?" she whispered.

His head tilted ever so slightly. "Go," was his echo-like answer. "This is what you dreamed about and what I'm offering you." For the second time, he sagged like a deflated balloon.

Edie glanced at the entrance, where bales of hay were erected. Pumpkins sat on top with candles flickering in the orange faces that ranged from scary to happy. They were the only light source besides the moon. The scent emanating from the fruit was delicious, even sans the spices Mom always added to the puree of pumpkin for the fall feast.

Edie held her position of one foot forward and the other back. There was the party, but if this wasn't a joke — and it was no joke because her heart told her so, and her heart was never wrong — she'd miss out on the greatest chance of her life.

She inched past the pumpkins and eased into the maze. When she glanced up, the moon remained high, casting light but also eerie shadows from the rows of dead corn.

If her biggest wish came true, she'd find herself back in time, living amongst her ancestors like an Ojibway maiden, being courted by a handsome brave, and given a wonderful, romantic life.

Yeah, right.

This had to be a joke. What if the people who'd decorated for the party had also set up the maze? She could see the looks on her friends' faces when she arrived for the dance, all laughing because she'd fallen for their trick instead of a treat.

The wind howled, chastising her.

Her mind was made up. She'd listen to the darned scarecrow, but if this was a joke . . .

She crept down the first row of the maze. The wind suddenly vanished. Not one husk fluttered. The only sound was her moccasins pressing on the worn grass beneath her feet. As she walked, she ran her palm along the dead stalks, anything to make a noise to break up the eerie silence. The stalks obeyed by making a rustling and crunching jangle.

She wet her lips. The wind had to be the Thunderbirds, and the being at the entrance must be *Mandaamin*, which was why he wouldn't answer her questions. He'd called her here, for if he hadn't, why hadn't the motorcyclist who'd passed her on the highway stopped to marvel at this phenomenon? What if the bike rider wasn't from here, though?

Damn, she should have checked his license plate. Then again, at the rate he'd been speeding, she hadn't had time to decipher if he was an American, since many from the States came to Morson for a weekend of fishing. Hmm, maybe she was wrong. The park owned by the Ojibway was closed, and every other tourist camp had called it a day for the season.

There wasn't much scent here, only the earth beneath her feet.

She walked farther, still running her palm along the dead stalks. As she took a turn here and another turn there in the labyrinth, what brushed her palm became richer, silkier. The corn was greener, too. Life. Even the scent was powerful — the fresh taste of maize on her tongue.

This was incredible. The beating of her heart was sheer excitement, ready to pop from her chest. She should call her friends and let them share her adventure, because this was no joke. Not in a million years could the tricksters at the party create this maze.

Yes, she'd call Tamara. Wait, she'd left her purse and cell phone in the car, along with her keys.

Oh shit. Someone could spy her vehicle from the road, turn into the path she'd followed, and take her car and belongings.

Edie whipped on her foot and retraced her steps. As she rushed through the walls of corn, the entrance refused to appear. She kept meeting walls of dead stalks.

Going farther in might lead to a secret way out.

Edie hustled in the other direction. She was on the right track. The stalks were no longer dead but growing greener. The scent of ripe corn settled under her nose. She darted around another corner and screeched to a halt.

What looked like flickering flames danced in front of an opening to an entrance, or some kind of portal. Vibrant colors of orange, red, and yellow rippled. This wasn't a fire, because the maze would have burned to a crisp.

The beat of Edie's jittering heart sped up another notch. If the thing kept pounding rapidly, she'd shoot to the full moon.

All she had to do was leap forward to find out if the scarecrow had spoken the truth.

CHAPTER TWO: WILDERNESS NOW

Edie squeezed her eyes shut, thrust out her hands, and shuffled into the mirage of rippling flames. Nothing scorched her skin. Only warmth surrounded her. Something feather-like seemed to stroke every inch of her flesh.

She kept walking, arms out and palms facing whatever awaited on the other side. The scent of spruce was present, even buttercups, and the fresh taste of water. Her feet trampled grass and leaves. A bird chirped. Maybe a chickadee, by its sad song. The little black-capped critters usually sang this tune in the early morning or evening.

Maybe she'd walked out of the maze.

Very slowly, she peeled open her lids to nature—everywhere. Spruce towered high above her. Underbrush shot up from the earth. Wild flowers were aplenty. Why, she could've been in the northwest of Ontario. The sun shone bright, its rays beating down on her. The heaviness of the doeskin dress was a tad hot on her skin.

"It is as my vision spoke. She will walk through the flames to join me . . ."

A man's voice whirled into Edie's thoughts. No, not her thoughts. His rich tone lovelier than a song had penetrated her eardrums. Nor had he spoken English, but Ojibway, and not the *Anishinaabemowin* she studied in class. Koko called the language Great-Grandpa had interpreted for the courts the old language. Even stranger, she understood him.

"*Ishkode-kwe,*" he whispered.

Edie blinked. He'd called her Fire Woman. "I . . . I . . ."

10

Oh, heaven help her, standing beside the bush of green where buttercups sprung was the very man who'd haunted her dreams since childhood. His bronzed, long, strong fingers grasped the stems of flowers—the very same hands that had always reached across the mist to her.

Hair darker than a moonless sky was braided into two plaits and parted down the middle. His nose was long and sharp. Eyes that matched the hue of his hair were narrow in shape. Cheekbones capable of cutting diamonds sat high on his oblong face. Lips the shade of poppies, yet very slim, were pursed in a questioning pucker. Never had she drunk in such a gorgeous specimen of the male persuasion before. Machismo seemed to emanate from him.

No. Wait. Wrong word. He wasn't some macho guy like the boys at university. Courage, strength, and bravery sprang from his athletic body. His masculinity originated from the confidence in his straight posture, hard abs, and forward stare.

Again, he held out his offering.

"I'm ... I'm not supposed to be here ..." Just as Edie smoothed her dress, she slapped her hand over her mouth. She'd spoken the old language. They could communicate. The scarecrow hadn't been a joke or a mirage. This was real. Realer than ...

She pinched the back of her hand and winced from the sharp prick.

"Yes, you are to be here." He curiously peered at her hand, no doubt thinking she was insane for intentionally hurting herself. "The Thunderbirds willed this, for it stormed during my entire quest."

"Wh-what?" she sputtered. He'd had a vision about her, just as she'd dreamed about him? "That wasn't a scarecrow. It was *Mandaamin*."

"You speak of our corn spirit?" He tilted his head.

"I'm . . . I was going to a Halloween party. There was a corn maze. A scarecrow. All kinds of . . ." She stopped. He'd have no clue what any of that was, and her interpretation from English to Ojibway had sounded weird, because she'd had to reference Halloween as the *fun night of the dead* – it was taboo to talk about in her culture of those who'd passed, much less have a party. Calling a scarecrow *the man made from grass* must have also stumped him.

"Fun night of the dead?" He peered. "Grass man? Lost in the corn?"

"I'm . . . I'm not from here." She pointed behind her while swiveling to the vanished dancing flames.

"No, you are not. I know so." He hedged in closer. His mouth moved into a slight curve. "Are you not going to accept my offering?"

"I . . . uh . . . um . . ." She reached out and clutched the bouquet. No man had ever gifted her with flowers before, much less upon meeting her. She couldn't help herself and brought the buttercups up to her nose and sniffed. "*Meegwetch.*"

He nodded, his lips still curved in a welcoming smile. Then he tapped his chest. "I am *Nimkii Makwa.*"

Thunder Bear. No wonder there'd been a storm during his quest. She licked her lips. "I'm Edie."

Slowly, he shook his head back and forth. "*Ishkode-kwe.*"

It was only appropriate he thought of her as Fire Woman, because she had appeared to him through the flames of the maze. Or maybe he saw her as Fire Woman in his vision. "Where are we?"

"*Pikwedina Sagainan.*"

Edie shuddered. He'd named the southern part of Lake of the Woods, just as she'd studied in class, because her people had previously divided the massive lake into four parts. They were at the water of the sandhills. Summer was upon them. His band was probably camped somewhere close by, maybe an hour's walk from the corn maze. As her studies had taught her, come fall, they'd split into individual family units to harvest the wild rice. Then they'd set off within the interior to escape the cold of winter.

"This is—this is . . . amazing."

The same curiousness appeared in his gaze, even a twinkling of amusement. "Come." He extended his hand. His gaze again flecked her over, eyes peculiarly glittering and pinned on the beads of her dress.

Heat clambered onto Edie's face. What was the exact century? He probably didn't know plastic existed. The beads traded for furs during the height of Canada's Fur Trade were probably glass or some other kind of material—that was if the French had crossed the Atlantic.

"You must hide those." He pointed at her dress. "The stitching isn't correct, but it will do." He stared at her moccasins.

Edie gaped at him. His actions said he was aware she wasn't from here, yet his suggestion also implied he was also fully aware she wasn't from his time period.

She stood, allowing him to remove the beads from her Halloween costume. How smart of him to rid her of anything that might alert his band of what had yet to be created. Even wilder, the plastic didn't disturb him or send him scurrying away.

The scent of the outdoors and sage drifted under her nose from his glistening skin, no doubt slathered in bear grease to deter the bugs. He sat on his haunches, still removing the beads.

She'd need bear grease out here. Already, bugs had picked up her unprotected skin and buzzed around. From what she could recall when she was last in this area, the black flies had been relentless while swimming on the beach at the bonfire party. She couldn't very well walk down to the store in

Morson and ask for insect repellent, either. The little town might not exist.

Thunder Bear used a fallen branch to dig a hole. He scooped up the beads he'd removed and planted them in the earth. Using the branch, he pushed the dirt over the beads and buried them. "Done." He stood, smacking his hands together to shake off the brown dirt on his palms and fingers.

"Come." He motioned at the animal path he'd probably used to reach his earlier destination.

Animal paths were something Shoomis had first taught Edie about while growing up. The four-legged creatures were the teachers, just as the books said. The Ojibway probably had a few trails out here, learned from the deer and other wildlife who trampled homemade paths throughout the summer and winter to navigate the thick bush.

Still clutching her flowers, she followed him.

"Braid your hair." His words weren't an order. The warmth of his voice hinted he was advising her.

"Here." She held out the flowers. "Hold these."

He stopped.

The breechclout barely covered his strong thighs. Leggings wouldn't be of use to him until the weather grew colder.

Thank goodness she kept her long locks waist length. If she'd broken through the maze portal with a contemporary haircut, people would have thought of her as crazy, in mourning, or having been fevered. Once she had two plaits braided, she tore a couple of fringes from the bottom of her dress to tie them.

"How did you know I would . . . well . . ." Too many questions swam through her mind.

"I told you already. The Thunderbirds came to me." He commenced walking.

His moccasin-covered feet barely skimmed the grass and leaves they trod over.

"Don't you have questions for me?" She pushed aside branches, almost recoiling at them. Wood ticks would be out. What if she ended up crawling in the parasitic creatures who loved sitting in the trees and brush, waiting for something or someone to come by to latch on to?

He again ceased walking and pivoted with the grace of a buck trotting through the grass. "My questions were already answered—a long time ago."

His vision quest—what all young boys engaged in at around twelve years old to seek their true path—had no doubt answered them. Edie drew the flowers closer to her. How much did he know about her, exactly?

"There are two people I wish to introduce you to."

She had no choice but to follow, because he was guiding them through the bush again. In an attempt to gauge the time period, she asked "Are there fur traders?"

He nodded. "Yes, the Great Father who lives across the saltwater sent his people here." He halted and glanced over his strong shoulder. "Many have befriended them."

Maybe the century was the late eighteenth or early nineteenth then.

"They also trap the furs." He pressed his lips together. "They do not honor the cycle of life. That is why they have sent their own people in to obtain the fur from the animals. They feel we are not providing them with enough to sustain their desire for the pelts." His eyes tilted downward in wariness. "You must be careful."

"Careful?"

"Some have taken our women as wives. As I said, they are our friends, but be careful."

She hadn't travelled time to end up a French fur trader's wife. Unease spooked her spine. She hedged in closer to Thunder Bear. "What about wood ticks?" she whispered.

His slim lips almost stretched to his ears. "I am walking

first, am I not?"

"Yes."

"This means they will jump on me, not you. I am protected. Therefore, they will slip from me, and not cling."

If Edie's face got any hotter, she'd match the dancing flames of the maze. "Thank you."

"You don't need to thank me. This is what a man does for . . . others."

Something glistened in his eyes she couldn't read, but the way he'd paused meant he was doing this for her because he already thought of her as his . . . woman.

"Come. We have a long walk ahead of us." He resumed his graceful stride.

The heat cloyed at Edie. Right about now she could use her tank top, pair of shorts, and sandals. "Have they constructed forts?" If the French had, then the area had been truly explored.

"The traders of fur?"

"Yes."

Thunder Bear nodded. "After we harvest the wild rice, I will begin laying my traps."

"You won't stay in the winter camp?" This meant he'd venture far off somewhere to seek the animals to bring to one of the forts. In his younger days, Shoomis used to head out to his trapline and trade in his pelts at the local Hudson Bay.

"It must be done. Especially now that you are here."

Again, a shiver spooked her spine. " . . . now that I'm here?"

"Yes." His voice had firmed. "You will be safe. I am taking you to the people who have waited for your arrival."

"Somebody's waiting for me?" Edie couldn't help her sputter.

"Walks with a Limp and Woman of the Sky lost their daughter last spring. They will welcome your presence, for they know you are a gift from *Gitche Manidoo*."

Simultaneously, Edie's heart brightened yet darkened—happy she'd have a place to stay, but sad two people had lost their child. She could only imagine the grief consuming them.

She halted. What would Mom and Dad say? Or Shoomis and Koko? Her friends? Her brothers and sister? How long could she stay here before her family panicked and wondered if she'd become another murdered and missing Indigenous woman, a horrible plight that was ravishing the native population of Canada?

"I . . . I . . . ." She must go back.

"Did *Gitche Manidoo* will this?" He stopped and folded his arms across his strong, bronzed chest meant for a woman to lay her hand or head.

"I don't know." The panic was expanding through her racing blood.

"Did He not use *Mandaamin* to send you here?"

"I don't know." The frustration and fright climbing up her legs threatened to ignite her heart into little pieces. "I have family far away. Friends."

"You will be fine. They will be fine." He reached out. His finger dusted her chin. The soft tip, although rough from laborious work, was velvet on her skin. His dark eyes looked deep into her, as if catching her soul in the palm of his hand.

"I can stay . . . for a while." The saliva in her mouth drained away. No matter that a blackfly buzzed around her head, she couldn't move or drag her stare away from Thunder Bear's potent gaze.

"Trust me?" He quirked a sleek black brow.

"Y-yes."

"Come, then." He wrapped his fingers around her hand that wasn't holding the flowers.

Incredible strength, yet also gentleness, cloaked his grip. She was led along, as if they were floating slightly above the grass trampled by the animals. While she was smacked by branches, he easily stalked around the boughs of spruce.

Blue jays squawked. Robins sang. Chickadees made their *dee-dee* sound. An oriole whistled. The bush was alive with smell and sound. The black flies continued to buzz around her head, but they didn't attempt to bite her.

Trying to walk as lightly as he did became easier by simply following his movements, which allowed her to almost dance through the forest. Even though her breathing came heavy, his couldn't be heard. Living as he did, he was most likely used to walking long stretches, especially in snowshoes — which wasn't an easy feat — in the winter.

The flexing of his strong back muscles and shoulders didn't come from dumbbells or weights. Being one with nature had molded and shaped his body into a physique the gym rats back in Winnipeg would envy. The food he ate also played a vital role in the stamina he possessed. He didn't know what cane sugar was, either, or maybe he did if fur traders had infiltrated the region. His nourishment was protein and fiber from the animal meat and plant life.

No wonder so many *Anishinaabeg* suffered from type two diabetes now. They were deprived of what had sustained them for millennia, having changed their diet too fast, like the snapping of fingers. The same for alcoholism. The poisonous drink was devastating the People and reserves.

A thick weight seemed to sit on Edie's chest. She couldn't believe she longed to weep for what the People had lost — what she'd lost. As Thunder Bear had told her, *Gitche Manidoo* willed her arrival. The maze hadn't been a fluke. The scarecrow had been *Mandaamin*. Maybe she was here to acquire knowledge to share with her own in the present day.

"Ever since my vision quest, I have waited where I was directed to stand. I knew you would come," he softly said.

The thickness on Edie's chest vanished. She let him lead

her along. Given the relaxation of his shoulders, and the odd turn of his head when he'd glance her way smiling, he was simply content to walk. She had to remember the golden rule of silence she'd learned — general chitchat wasn't something her ancestors had engaged in, because they were believers in carefully choosing their words before allowing anything to spill from their mouths, since what was said could not be recalled.

There were so many questions she wished to ask, but patience was also a virtue of her ancestors, just like the predator waiting hours in its hiding place for prey to arrive and pounce on, or wolves working together to tirelessly chase down a deer, running the poor creature to death before its eventual surrender.

She shuddered . . . a predator hunting its prey. Was she prey? Did Thunder Bear plan on using the utmost patience to capture her?

CHAPTER THREE: SWEET SALVATION

About an hour into their walk of silence, with Thunder Bear continuing to glance over his strong shoulder to offer a warm yet sensual smile, splashing carried to them. Laughter. Voices of children and adults. They were closing in upon the village.

In moments, Edie would meet the people she'd read about and studied in university.

They stepped through the thickness of the forest to the beach where she'd swum three years ago. This wasn't the exact spot, though. The smooth sand was alive with people who washed clothing or paddled their canoes out in the water. Naked children ran along the shoreline, chasing each other and kicking up wet sand.

The noise and motion came to a full stop. Everyone stared — at her.

Edie swallowed.

Thunder Bear tightened his grip on her fingers. "Come. This way." He led her to the shoreline. "You must wash your face first or they will wonder about the paint you are wearing."

Her makeup.

He released his fingers from hers.

A smidgen of disappointment sat in Edie's tummy. Although the sun was rising higher and the heat was becoming thicker, the warmth their touching skin had generated, even the sweat on their palms, had been as cozy as sitting around a bonfire wrapped in a blanket.

Edie handed him her flowers. A twinkle sparkled in his eyes. He held the buttercups and motioned at the water.

"Thank you." She squatted. Water coming in from the lake lapped at the sand beneath her moccasins. The fringes of her dress received a dunking. She splashed the refreshing liquid onto her face, but all she did was move her makeup around. A cloth of some kind was required.

"The sand." Thunder Bear pointed. "Use the sand."

Sand to wash her face? How silly. Wait, maybe she was the silly one? Shoomis, if enjoying a shore lunch while fishing, always scrubbed the cast-iron frying pan using sand. The second the gritty stuff met her skin, her flesh seemed to pop in approval. She scrubbed and experienced the cleanliness no exfoliator she'd bought had ever produced. To rinse off what had become wet muck, again she splashed more water on her face.

There was one problem. Her mascara remained intact.

"Rub here." Thunder Bear tapped his thigh. "The bear grease will help remove what you painted on your lashes."

Edie touched his leg. Having her fingers on the muscle of his quad twitching beneath was pure heat ready to burn her skin. If she didn't keep her balance, she'd fall over with a big splash. Shakily, she applied the greasy material to her lashes. When she rinsed off her eyes, the mascara was gone, just as petroleum jelly did the trick in the twenty-first century.

Using the hem of her dress, hands still shaking, she patted her face dry. The doeskin material was soothing and soft.

"Come." He again offered his open palm.

Her fingers, seeming to have a life of their own, practically jumped from their connected spots on her hand and clamped around his, as if demanding to touch him of their own accord.

The stares from the people resumed. A hint of shyness crept along Edie's skin. She clutched the flowers tighter.

"They are over there." Thunder Bear puckered his lips in

the direction where the lodges were erected. "I think they will be delighted to meet you."

He must be speaking about the couple who'd lost their daughter.

Many stunning maidens gawked. Naturally, their admiring gazes lingered on Thunder Bear. At his age, he should've been already married with a family. The maidens were probably around fifteen or sixteen, most likely being courted, since that was the eligible age for girls. Edie would be considered a little old, but that didn't mean she was on the shelf or anything. Some did marry later.

Of course the girls' dresses were sleeveless for the summer, because the traditional dress possessed detachable arms. Not so for her. No wonder she was receiving curious glances.

Thunder Bear led her into the main part of the camp. As she'd learned from her studies, the dome-shaped wigwams were covered in birch bark and erected on a slight slope to fend off water when the sky opened up to let down a good rain. Some ladies smoked meat. Others worked with their babies in the moss bags.

They stopped at one wigwam where an older man sat outside on a mat fashioned from the reeds of bulrushes.

"Walks with a Limp, this is Fire Woman. She is new to the camp and a person I have been waiting for," Thunder Bear announced. "She comes from a place far away but was instructed by *Mandaamin* to find us."

The older man's eyes crinkled. He was handsome, his skin still smooth. He must be in his late thirties, since he'd probably had his daughter when he was around twenty. "It is good to meet you. Thunder Bear is much admired in our camp. For him to bring a stranger among us sent by *Mandaamin* is a good sign."

Walks with a Limp glanced over his shoulder. "Woman of the Sky. Thunder Bear has brought us a guest."

A woman with glossy black hair tied back vacated the wig-wam. Youthfulness danced in her dark eyes, slim lips, and glowed on her bronzed skin. Gauging her years wasn't easy, because most Ojibway women tended to appear younger than their true age. She was most likely in her mid-thirties.

"This is Fire Woman. Thunder Bear was instructed to bring her to our camp. She will be our guest." Walks with a Limp's command wasn't a terse order but a gentle instruction to his wife.

"A guest?" Woman of the Sky arched her black brow. "Then come. Eat." She extended her hand to the wigwam. "Drink. Your travel must have been a long one." She did peer curiously at Edie's dress.

Edie smoothed the front of the doeskin that should have had detachable sleeves. "Thank you." Accepting the offer of food and water was obligatory, even though she wasn't hungry, thanks to the butterflies still dancing in her belly.

Edie followed the woman inside the wigwam. The breath flew from her lungs. Everything was just as she'd studied. A fire pit in the center. A sleeping place of soft-looking furs. A rush mat for Woman of the Sky to do her light work. Another rush mat for Walks with a Limp to sit and attend to his chores. Edie could also stand at full height within the comfy confines of the curved poles.

The scent was marvelous — a combination of tanned hides, fresh birch, cedar, and the lovely aroma of the outdoors.

Woman of the Sky indicated for Edie to sit on one of the rush mats next to the unlit fire. The older woman went back outside. Maybe she had something simmering in the cooking fire next to the wigwam.

Edie couldn't stop glancing around at the different items hanging from the lodge poles. Several deerskin bags full of something. Walks with a Limp's pipe. Birch bark baskets. A copper kettle. She gasped. They *had* been trading with the

French or English, because her People constructed everything from nature. A flintlock musket. Her hand came over her mouth. In her studies, the Ojibway had been notorious owners of guns.

Hanging on another pole was a bandolier bag decorated with glass beads and ribbons. This had to be the eighteenth century, when the Ojibway prospered in this area during the fur trade. The guns were valuable for war against the Dakota who'd also coveted the Boreal forest of Northwestern Ontario, but they'd soon be driven out to Minnesota and the prairies. As for the pretty *gashkibidaagan* she'd first taken notice of, this was where the men stored their powder charges and balls for their muskets.

Woman of the Sky reappeared. She held a tin plate and tin cup. Naturally, Edie would be served food on something her people valued during this era. Just as where she was seated, facing the entrance of the lodge, showed the respect and honor her people revered.

She accepted the plate and cup. There was no cutlery. Using her fingers, she picked out the meat and vegetable portions. Woman of the Sky grabbed one of the deerskin bags off the pole. She seated herself with legs to the side and worked on crafting moccasins, an endless task, since the numerous treks through the woods wore down the footwear and a new pair always needed to be on hand.

Edie tipped the plate and drank the broth. To cleanse her mouth, she sipped the water. The refreshing liquid was also welcome from the growing heat of the day.

Woman of the Sky set aside her crafting and stood. She smiled and took the cup and plate. In seconds she returned, holding a small birch bark bowl. Gratefully, Edie took the water to rinse off her hands and dab around her mouth.

"Thank you," she murmured, keeping her head slightly low.

Woman of the Sky cast another of her smiles that could light the night sky. Out of politeness, she wouldn't ask questions, this Edie knew. The lovely woman was ensuring Edie was refreshed and relaxed. Funny how commonplace during her time period it was to forego the genteel hospitality offered to a weary traveler in this century. She couldn't see anyone extending her food and drink if she'd been in Winnipeg, a stranger entering someone's house.

Woman of the Sky took the bowl Edie had used. Again, she vanished from the wigwam. Moments later, she came back. "Get some rest. Your travel was long, from what Thunder Bear told us." She moved to the side of the wigwam and unrolled a blanket of fur.

Edie had arrived at the maze around eight in the evening, and after trekking through the bush, exhaustion should consume her, but tiredness wasn't present. Refusing the offer was deemed rude, though. She stood and made her way to the thick robe and lay on top. Something resembling a pillow was offered to her.

When Woman of the Sky vanished, Edie closed her eyes, forcing herself to sleep. But that was impossible, for she had no clue what would happen next.

Then again, there was the portal the scarecrow had told her she could always return to, especially if her excursion to the land of her ancestors became dangerous, such as the Dakota deciding to wage war the way they had for one hundred and fifty years in this area.

The creature had warned that once she leapt through the dancing flames, there'd be no returning to this peaceful place.

"Did she say where she comes from?" Walks with a Limp asked.

Thunder Bear could not reveal his vision to his older friend and mentor, because no man did, unless instructed by the *manidoog*, as he had been. But he was to only share part of his knowledge with Fire Woman. The most he could honestly say was, "She comes from a place far away. I have been expecting her. *Gitche Manidoo* willed this."

"I believe so." Walks with a Limp frowned. He stared off to where kids played in the sand. "My daughter walks in the spirit world, and Fire Woman has arrived . . ."

Woman of the Sky squatted by the fire outside the wigwam. She hummed a pretty song to match the chirps of the birds.

"Your wife seems quite content." Thunder Bear arched his brow.

"That she does." Walks with a Limp glanced over his shoulder. "She should have been Sings Like a Bird. I have not heard her sing ever since . . ." He puckered his thin lips.

Thunder Bear simply nodded, for they could not speak the names of those who had departed unless during ceremony.

"There is a time to mourn, and a time to live . . ." Walks with a Limp exhaled a big breath. "My daughter's husband, Big Cloud, has begun to live once more."

Again, Thunder Bear nodded. His mentor's son-in-law had paid his debt of one round of the seasons to his in-laws, as tradition instructed when parents lost a child who was married. During the spring, the tall, handsome brave had vacated their wigwam. Big Cloud was now courting another maiden to replace the loss of his wife. Just as their son-in-law knew when to move on, the parents must now do so, too.

From the constant humming and smiles from Woman of the Sky, it was clear she was ready to embrace what Creator had sent her in place of her lost daughter.

"Just as the cuts on her arms have healed over, so will her heart, but scars remain." Thunder Bear briefly glanced at the healed mutilations on the inner side of Woman of the Sky's forearms, where she'd taken a knife and had slashed herself upon hearing of her daughter's death. Her hair was growing back, now long enough to braid, since she'd also shorn her plaits.

"She rests." Woman of the Sky approached. "She is a pretty woman. Lovely. I sense no wickedness in her heart."

"There is none. This I have seen," Thunder Bear reassured them. "She is meant to be here."

"I prepared a proper place for her to sleep. Did she bring anything in her travels?" Woman of the Sky bent over the fire.

"No. Only what she wears, and she has much to learn, for she does not quite know all of our ways. She will need a teacher if she is to be my wife."

A small smile edged up the corners of Woman of the Sky's mouth. She patted Thunder Bear's arm. "That I can do."

"Thank you. I must go. Tell Fire Woman I will come by tonight." Thunder Bear stalked off to his own wigwam, where his parents resided.

Fire Woman was in good hands with his mentor and mentor's wife. Life would be extremely difficult for his soon-to-be bride, because she'd no doubt left behind many people she loved. Just by her actions, she was not of this world where he belonged, but he had a hunch she was strong and could withstand the trials and tribulations of what awaited her.

Edie rolled over on the soft furs. Sweat peppered her hairline and stuck to her backside. The heat had woken her. The time must be mid-afternoon, when the sun baked the land with its intense rays.

The wigwam wasn't dark, but not bright either. Woman of the Sky was working on her crafting. She sat by the empty fire pit.

The words *What time is it?* were on the tip of Edie's tongue.

27

Asking was moot. The People didn't live by the white man's clock as she did, something she'd have to get used to. Nor was her cellphone at her side to check text messages from friends.

She sat up.

"Did you get enough rest?" Woman of the Sky kept stitching away.

"Yes. The heat woke me." Edie smoothed her dress. For some weird reason, she should feel uncomfortable waking in a strange place. The coziness of the birch bark covering the lodge was as soothing as a cool blanket to expunge the perspiration the sun had caused.

"It is a little late to wash yourself, but come. We will go to the water where you can bathe." Woman of the Sky rolled up whatever she was working on and tucked it into one of the deerskin bags.

She reached for another bag from the pole and stood.

Edie rose off her bed of fur and followed Woman of the Sky from the wigwam. The children still played. Most of the women had vanished. Being so hot, and the days long, the People were probably at rest and would liven up once it cooled some.

A time to play. A time to work. A time to rest. They truly did follow nature's teachings.

"The blueberries are ripe. I have been gathering them." Woman of the Sky led them to the shoreline.

A welcoming gentle breeze was refreshing under the midday sun. "I can help, if you want." After all the older lady had done for Edie, offering assistance was a must.

The suggestion had been the right thing to say, because Woman of the Sky's closed-mouth gentle smile said she was thankful for the help. No doubt her daughter had once assisted her with the many tasks.

Once Edie bathed, she could hardly wait to dive into her new life.

Chapter Four: He Sells Sanctuary

Washing took place at the lake. First, the birchbark containers and tinware had to be scraped off and rinsed at the wigwam to not sour the water where they drank from and bathed. Then they had to haul everything down to the beach to begin the cleaning process.

Just a gentle mixture of sand and water was used, so as to not strain the precious bark. The white man's plates could receive a vigorous scouring, Woman of the Sky had instructed.

"Are clothes washed the same way?" Edie knelt in the sand, scrubbing one of the tin plates.

"They are carefully wiped down. If they require bear grease for softening, it is applied." Woman of the Sky had taken on the task of cleansing the birch bark bowls. "Then hung to air out the smells our bodies produce. Washing will ruin the tanned hides."

A hint of heat crept onto Edie's cheekbones. Of course. When had she ever washed leather in the twenty-first century? "What about teeth?"

"I took care of your teeth, but you left the twigs I offered in the bowl, and also the herb to freshen your breath." Woman of the Sky's giggle wasn't mocking, but one a mother used to chide her daughter.

Edie had to laugh, because toothpaste didn't exist out in the wilderness. Not being able to run a brush over her teeth left her tummy a tad squeamish. Considering the bones dug up of Indigenous People and their lack of cavities, the remedy must work.

"Is there some kind of brush I can make for my teeth?" Edie rinsed the sand off the plate. "And . . . uh . . . a paste?"

"Yes." Woman of the Sky nodded. "Anything is possible out here. The Great Mother is the one and only resource we require."

"Can you help me make one?"

"Of course." Woman of the Sky ducked her head and glanced back up. There was a shyness that wasn't present before. "I am glad Thunder Bear brought you here."

"I am, too." The chemistry between them was a thick robe of fur blanketing Edie's shoulders. She ached to reach over and hug the woman who'd suffered much, and while suffering, had offered Edie a roof over her head and food.

"You must be hot in a dress you cannot remove the sleeves from. You are welcome to wear one of mine until I teach you how to fashion your own." Woman of the Sky set aside the birch bark bowl and reached for another. The sunlight beat down on her black hair, giving her mane a blue cast.

To protest was considered rude, but goodness, the woman had already given so much to Edie. "Thank you very much. I am most humbled and grateful."

Woman of the Sky pursed her ruby-colored lips. "You are also most welcome to stay in our lodge for as long as you wish."

"I accept your generous offer." Edie sat straighter. "I will do my best to aid you in all of your tasks and chores. Consider me your helper."

"Yes . . . a helper." Wistfulness dusted Woman of the Sky's eyes. "It is good to have a woman in the lodge again." She wiped at her dress. "We must hurry. I think Thunder Bear will be visiting us tonight." Mischief twinkled in her gaze.

Thunder Bear left his lodge. He chewed on the sprig to cleanse his mouth, after earlier taking a pine needle to his teeth to clean in between. The sun had set. Fires lit the camp. Every now and then sparks shot into the air from someone throwing another log down, or poking at the burning wood in the pits.

Fire Woman should have settled in. Since she was older than most maidens, he could freely approach her, yet he could not be as forthcoming with his intentions as the Frenchmen of the forts were. To be so bold was considered rude, even an affront to his capability of wooing a female. As all braves, he had to rely on his reputation of honor, bravery, and courage to speak for him, unlike the traders of fur who used sweet words, flirtatious stares, and engaging conversation.

In his vision, the Thunderbirds had told him to expect a woman who'd seen nineteen summers. There was wisdom in Fire Woman's eyes most maidens lacked, for they hadn't lived long enough yet to experience life, having been confined to the safety of the women in their family. Not the same for the lady of his vision quest. Instinct told him Fire Woman had lived on her own, had traveled unescorted on her own, and was well educated in the ways of the white man.

Her accent gave her away. She didn't have the smooth speech when communicating in her mother tongue. There was a sharpness to her words associated with those who served the Queen Mother from the east. Those who served the King Father had a rolling *rrrrr* to their tongues, but their words were music, not the bold straight lines of the men who belonged to the Queen Mother.

He had many furs to trap when *Biboon* woke from his cold slumber to reign his harsh breath of snow and wind on the land. Fire Woman must learn how to prepare the pelts for trade if they were to marry and have their own home to raise their children in. She must be made to understand the importance of where she belonged in the circle, and the importance of the continuance of the circle.

His ancestors before him had first encountered the white man and hadn't relied on the materials received by trade. As for him, he'd been shown from a young age how to trap and the best places to take his furs to receive the guns.

He stopped at Walks with a Limp's wigwam. Nobody was outside, so he tapped on the birch covering of the lodge.

"Enter," Walks with a Limp called out.

Thunder Bear poked his head in. Fire Woman sat by the empty pit. Her hands fumbled at the mending Woman of the Sky had probably instructed her on. The light in Fire Woman's eyes and her big smile said she was glad to see him. Most maidens ducked their heads, but not her.

"I was wondering if you would like to take a walk. The night is warm, and Grandmother Moon is awake."

Fire Woman glanced at Woman of the Sky, who nodded her approval.

Fire Woman set the deerskin in the bag and hung it on one of the lodge poles. She smoothed her new dress that bared her toned arms and stood. She cast a nervous smile and followed Thunder Bear from the wigwam.

"I thought you would play your flute." There was a hint of a chuckle to her words.

Thunder Bear had never bothered to construct one, for he knew there had been no reason to after his vision quest. "Those are for maidens who have only seen fifteen or sixteen summers. I thought you would prefer to walk instead." He motioned at the beach.

"You have never questioned me about where I come from." She folded her arms. Her hair was brushed out and flowed down her back and to her waist, just as he'd experienced after she'd emerged from the fiery waves in the bush.

"I know already. It is a place far away."

"It is a place far ahead, very far ahead. You will never see it." She glanced at him.

He kept in step with her. "Maybe I will." He arched his brow. "You do not know this. You have not seen what I saw."

"What did you see?" A hint of fear mixed with the curiosity in her delicate voice.

"That you are born for this, as I was born for this."

"Do you mean this is meant to happen?" She stopped.

The waves gently rolling into the sand carried to where they stood. Light from the moon reflected off the vast expanse of *Pikwedina Sagainan*.

"Yes, I do." The tips of his fingers urged him to stroke her face that was finer and smoother-looking than the most precisely tanned hide. As luxurious as what the white man called *silk*. "I saw the dancing flames you came from."

Her oval-shaped eyes rounded. "You—you did?"

He nodded. "Fire Woman. Is it not an appropriate name? The flames did not burn you. Fire is your friend. Your spirit guide."

"I want to be honest." She wet her plush mouth with the color riper than raspberries. "I have been educated in the ways of the white men. Where I come from, we live like white men."

"I know you do. It is in your speech, your movement, your behavior." He reached out and touched her bare arm that possessed delicate strength beneath the smooth flesh he palmed. "You are here to become what you are meant to truly be. We will teach you, if you are willing."

"I am more than willing. In the white man's world, I am learning everything about the People. I have studied the People ever since I was a little girl."

"I know you have. It is why you came." He could not resist letting his palm move along her arm. Beneath the skin he stroked, her slight muscle flexed.

She wet her lips.

The urge to claim her mouth was a test of his restraint.

They'd only met this morning, and he must go slow. To slide his mouth over hers after just meeting was not how a warrior conducted himself. Yet, the way she'd drew her tongue along her lower lip was caressing and licking him beneath his breechclout. Her innocent gesture might as well have been her nails raking his backside, her hands boldly exploring his arms, and her breasts melting against his chest.

She was aptly named, because a fire danced in her sparkling dark eyes. A fire of desire. A fire of need. A fire flickering with mesmerization in her gaze touching his face.

He stifled the groan aching to leave his throat.

She seemed to drag her gaze to the dark water. If where they stood was better lit, he'd probably witness redness on her cheeks.

"What is it?"

Again, she wet her lips. "I . . . Maybe I should go back?"

A punch seemed to knock his gut. "Return? Now?"

"No." She shook her head. "I mean the wigwam. Not the . . . the . . ."

"The dancing flames?"

She nodded.

Relief loosened the knots of his shoulder muscles. He didn't believe in restraining any maiden, but if she had dared to run for where she had come from, he probably would have tossed her over his shoulder and carted her back to the camp. Now that he had found what he'd waited twelve years to capture, he wasn't letting her go.

Somehow, he had to help her find her courage to survive with them. She was destined to be here.

Edie was treading in dangerous waters. If she let herself become lost in Thunder Bear's potent gaze, there'd be no returning to where she truly belonged — in the present day of the twenty-first century. She'd never see her parents, brothers, or sister again. Her friends. The university. But her gut kept telling her she belonged here.

The way Thunder Bear studied her face told her he ached to take her in his arms and kiss her. To allow him to claim her lips was a definite no. One kiss would lead to the unthinkable, and she wasn't ready to decide if she should stay or leave. So far, she wasn't missing the comforts of home. Soon, she would. Once summer left and fall blanketed the land, she'd have to endure pure harshness, maybe even starvation.

She shuddered. The professor at the university and her great-grandfather had proclaimed that during the lean winter months, if the animals hid, the People had boiled their moccasins and scraped and ate bark to stave off starvation, for an empty belly turned people into *wiindigoog*. Although she didn't believe in the *wiindigo*, there had to be a reason the cannibalistic monster belonged to Ojibway folklore. Or maybe folklore didn't exist? Maybe the old stories were true?

"Your thoughts race," Thunder Bear murmured. He kept stroking her bare arm. "Put them to rest. We live in the day, not the tomorrow."

He was right. If Edie was going to make this the most amazing experience she'd dreamed about, she must remain focused.

"Do not let fear guide you. Fear is your enemy. Here, you will learn to put your fear at rest." He spoke in a reassuring tone. The velvet of his voice was his graceful yet strong hands rubbing her shoulders in reassurance.

Although she shouldn't, Edie inched toward him, closing the slight gap between them. She wrapped his lean waist and laid her head on his strong chest. His palm rested on the back of her head. He stroked ever so slightly. His free arm wrapped her waist.

"Fire Woman," he whispered. His words steamed the top

of her head. "Do not be fearful. I will take good care of you. This I vow."

"I know you will." When she spoke, her lips brushed his nipple accidently, a hard piece of flesh alive, as if waiting to be gently pecked or suckled.

"Come, there is still much to see." His fingers grazed her back with reassuring strokes. "We will walk."

"I'd like that." Yet being enclosed in his embrace was the sanctuary she'd sought from childhood. As much as she loved her parents and grandparents, this was the first time she'd experienced such protection, as if he'd give up his own life for a stranger who he'd only met hours ago.

She had to force herself from his embrace. His arms slid from her, but his hands touched her hips before falling to his sides. His Adam's apple shifted. Maybe he felt the same way about the disruption to their clinch.

She tangled her fingers in his.

Curiosity flickered in his stare.

"Where I come from, we hold hands. It is a gesture we use with people we like."

His bared straight white teeth flashing from his full smile told Edie he was amused.

"We walk this way with a boyfriend."

"Boyfriend?"

"A suitor."

"Ah, I see. This is rather nice." He increased the pressure of their entwined fingers. "This is only done to guide someone, as I did for you this morning, but to simply walk this way . . . yes, very nice."

"If we feel playful, we swing them back and forth." She swung their locked hands as they strolled the beach. Her moccasins and the sand beneath them became one.

"Like a game." His chuckle was as lyrical as his speech. Sweet music to her ears.

"I guess it could be perceived as a game."

"Have you done this with others?"

Edie ducked her head. "Once."

"Yes?"

"He was a boy . . ." How to formulate the right words in Ojibway? "During puberty, we were more than friends. Since he was a boy, he was called a boyfriend. Which means we were very close and shared kisses."

He quirked a brow.

"But . . . I . . . you know why I am here."

"Yes, I told you already. *Gitche Manidoo* willed this to happen. The Thunderbirds shared with me during my vision quest what I am to do."

She peeked at him then glanced away. There was more he'd seen than what he was telling her, but she wouldn't press him. Out here, patience was a virtue. "I was too obsessed with my ancestors. My mom chastised me for romanticizing the past. She kept telling me life was much harsher and more difficult than what I was daydreaming about. She used Shoomis and Koko as an example. They almost lived as you do. But they resided in dwellings like the forts you encounter."

Thunder Bear nodded. "She was wrong about life being hard. Life is only difficult when you cannot accept what is Creator's will."

What he said was true. Shoomis and Koko said the same. She used her chin to motion at the bear claws strung around his neck. Maybe he could share about that. "What about your necklace. It's beautiful."

"This was a gift from my spirit guide." He touched the necklace. "My first hunt. I was sixteen summers."

She shivered, for something was coming, a deep story she sensed by the tone of his voice.

"This . . ." He drew a line down the jagged scar on his chest. " . . . is my mark from *makwa*. I woke him during his sleep."

"He was hibernating?"

Thunder Bear nodded. "I came across him — what I thought to be at the time, an accident, for to wake one during a deep sleep where he's burrowed in his hole beneath the snow always results in danger. If woken, there is the possibility he might not return to sleep, and he will succumb to his hunger. Other times, he will be angry. For me, he was very angry."

She held her breath.

"I was still learning my craft. By the time I'd notched my arrow, he came at me. He . . . he clawed me across the chest. I felt it on my breastbone and fell backward. Being my spirit guide, he paused before his full attack, as if giving me a fighting chance. I was able to fire my arrow into his heart." His jaw tensed. He looked out to the lake, a silver glow beneath the moon. "I had to use five to take him down. He was that strong."

He shook back his braids that had fallen forward. "I sang and danced for him."

Edie nodded. A hunter always prayed and sang for the four-legged, winged, or finned creatures for bravely giving up their lives so the People could live.

"I begged him for his strength and courage. He gave both to me. It is why I wear the necklace." He touched the one jagged claw. "He broke this on the rock when he crumbled over and went to the spirit world."

"It is a beautiful story. One you will pass on to your children." Pride filled Edie's entire being.

"Yes, my children . . ." He stopped walking and stared at her.

Chapter Five: Wake to Freedom

Edie rolled over on the plush furs. Hushed voices and movement had penetrated her sleep. Since their lodge faced the east, the sun streamed inside. Someone must have opened the flap.

This was like having to wake for classes when she'd rather stay in bed under the covers. However, her ancestors woke and retired by the daylight, so she sat up. There'd be no coffee to sip. As for breakfast, she'd have to make her own from scratch instead of grabbing a box of cereal from the cupboard and milk out of the fridge.

There was no day of the week, either. No time or alarm clock. There were months. Depending on the dialect, they were experiencing either the halfway summer moon or berry moon. Which was why Woman of the Sky was picking blueberries.

Nobody was present. Woman of the Sky and Walks with a Limp must have gone outside to start their chores. Edie had better join them. She refused to be a lazy, ungrateful guest. And she'd better start thinking in Ojibway instead of English.

When she popped out from the wigwam, Woman of the Sky waited. "Come." She extended her hand. "Let us clean up first."

Although Edie wouldn't experience a true shower, she could enjoy a nice bath. At this early hour, the sun wasn't present to warm the lake. Maybe that was what she needed. A cool invigorating dunk to get her blood flowing.

Other females in the camp had the same idea and were

already at the beach scrubbing for the day. During their walk, Woman of the Sky had informed Edie the men bathed in a different area.

One maiden in particular stood out. She rubbed sand along her bare skin, her lithe body submerged almost to her breasts of lush mounds Edie could only produce with a push-up bra. Moisture beaded down the girl's skin, and her long, blue-black hair floated around her.

Woman of the Sky must have noticed Edie's appreciative stare, because she said, "That is Song Sparrow. She and her mother must have returned late from blueberry picking yesterday."

"She is stunning." Edie almost exclaimed *she could be a model in my world.*

"Yes, very stunning. Many expected . . ." Woman of the Sky shrugged. "Come."

"You were going to say something." Edie set down her belongings on a smooth rock jutting out from the sand.

"It does not matter. You are here now. And he took you for a walk last night." Woman of the Sky removed her dress. She placed the deerskin garment on the rock Edie had used.

Does not matter meant something more than what Woman of the Sky was letting on. "Tell me, please." Edie used her most polite tone.

"I do not wish to alarm you." The older woman gently touched Edie's bare arm.

Everything about Edie's new life was alarming. One more fly floating in her soup was moot. "Please, tell me," she again requested.

"Let me simply say she is quite enamored with Thunder Bear." The sunlight shone down on Woman of the Sky's face, which possessed only slight hints of crows' feet around her dark eyes. Being outside her whole life but protected by the bear grease, had most likely kept her skin supple.

"Were they . . . was he . . ." Dating wasn't the appropriate word. "Courting?"

"No." Woman of the Sky motioned to get in. She waded into the water. "Thunder Bear has courted no one."

Then what he'd told her was true about waiting for her arrival. A shiver spooked Edie's spine. The knocking of her knees wasn't from the cold liquid surrounding her calves, either.

"Each summer he left on his own," Woman of the Sky continued on. "He never said where he was going, but he would leave us for a good time."

To wait for me. Edie submerged herself beneath the surface. The water wrapped her skin. Her flowing blood galloped through her veins.

They were destined for each other. Maybe she *had* been born for this.

The sound of the paddle stroking through the water was a sweet lullaby. They were out in the open water, heading for one of the many islands to pick blueberries. Edie had a good hunch where she was. The massive island to her left was Bigsby Island where her paternal great-grandmother had been born. To witness everything without man-made construction, but as natural as nature had made this land, was amazing.

The worst part was, she couldn't share her knowledge with Woman of the Sky — tell her about what the earth had become now, the lake full of speeding boats polluting its waters, tourist camps everywhere, and an invisible line drawn down the massive lake, one side belonging to Canada and the other to the US.

Two other canoes followed behind.

Song Sparrow knelt gracefully at the bow of the first canoe while her mother steered.

Edie's heart clenched. In time, she'd return to her family. Thunder Bear should consider marrying Song Sparrow. While bathing earlier, the other maidens had surrounded the beautiful *Anishinaabe-kwe*, eager to inform her of the latest happenings at the camp while she had been gone. Then they had pointed at Edie.

Ten minutes later, they rolled up to the shoreline to the beach. Edie helped Woman of the Sky bring in the light canoe. She reached inside and gathered the birchbark bowls she'd use for picking the blueberries.

The other women joined them.

Song Sparrow approached. Her hips swayed. The fringes of her dress danced in movement with her elegant gait.

Edie pressed the two big bowls against her.

"Good morning," Song Sparrow called out. "I did not get to meet you. I am Song Sparrow. I am told Thunder Bear brought you to our camp." Her gaze was warm. Her shoulders relaxed.

Edie's stiffening spine became a hint of mellowness. "It is good to meet you, as well. I am Fire Woman."

"You are the guest of Woman of the Sky and Walks with a Limp." Song Sparrow kept walking but motioned at Edie to join her. "My friends told me you have much to learn."

Heat clambered onto Edie's face. She fell in step beside Song Sparrow. "Yes, I do. I come from a place that is very much a white man's settlement."

"You were born there?" Curiosity flickered in Song Sparrow's gaze.

"Yes."

"How did that come to be?" Song Sparrow led them into the abundance of black spruce.

"I . . . I . . . my family had a settlement close by." The lie had twisted Edie's tongue. She wasn't one for fibbing and had to steal peeks to see if Song Sparrow believed her.

"We are here to help." Song Sparrow took them further in. "Thunder Bear brought you, did he not?"

"Y-yes, he did."

Although Song Sparrow glided through the thick branches and just-as-thick underbrush, Edie couldn't stop stumbling and shooing away the boughs stretching out to her that were most likely full of the dreaded wood ticks. Thank goodness she'd braided her hair, or the bloodsucking parasites would be crawling all over her scalp.

About ten minutes later, Song Sparrow finally halted at a spot ripe with blueberries that weren't part of a breeding project to make them enormous like the ones found in a grocery store, but naturally grown by the Great Mother.

Unable to help herself, Edie picked one and slid the berry between her lips. The delicious sweetness and fresh taste were nothing her tongue had ever sampled before, even when berry-picking with Koko.

"Very good?" Song Sparrow giggled, revealing the maiden hiding beneath the mature woman she'd presented earlier. She snatched a sprig. Using her teeth, she picked the berries clean.

"The best berries I have ever tasted." Edie couldn't help sampling a sprig of her own.

"They are delicious with anything." Song Sparrow popped another one into her mouth. She went back to picking, adding berry after berry to her basket.

A few moments later, her seductive voice interrupted the chirps of the birds. "Thunder Bear took you for a walk last night."

Edie stopped picking the berries. She glanced at Song Sparrow.

"You are lucky to be able to be alone with him. This is my eighteenth summer. I wish my parents would allow me the same freedom. Mother will not." Song Sparrow's delicate shoulders slumped.

"Eighteen?" Goodness, the maiden would be a high school graduate starting her first year of university in the fall in Edie's world. "Really? I thought you were—" Was it insulting for her to point out she'd assumed Song Sparrow was younger because she was unmarried?

"Because I am not married?" A smidgen of a sly smile poked up Song Sparrow's curving mouth.

Edie searched her thoughts to ensure tact was in her reply. "You are very beautiful. Forgive me for assuming—"

"There is nothing to forgive." Song Sparrow resumed picking berries. "It is my choice not to marry . . . for now." She glanced at Edie. "We will be friends then?"

"Yes. Friends." Edie breathed a sigh. She sure could use a friend.

"I knew he was waiting for someone." Song Sparrow kept picking away. She broke off another sprig and ate a few blueberries. "I guessed correctly. He was waiting for you."

A flicker of embarrassment claimed Edie's face. "I would not say he—"

"But he was." Song Sparrow held a sprig. She again gazed at Edie. "That is fine with me. If this is Creator's will, then it is His will. I know He has something else planned for me."

Edie's mouth fell open. Such wisdom for one so young. Then again, eighteen in the eighteenth century wasn't the same as in the twenty-first century, where young adults were coddled like babies. Out here in the wilderness, one had to grow up fast. The spirituality the people possessed also added to their youthful wisdom. When Song Sparrow had her first moon time, she'd most likely been directed to the bush to contemplate her path on the red road during her flow.

"I . . ." Edie didn't want to be responsible for crushing a budding romance. Yet, even after only meeting Thunder Bear, having him pursuing someone else left a knot in her stomach.

"I can help you. I know Woman of the Sky has also been helping you." Song Sparrow set more blueberries into her container.

Everyone was so generous. Guilt poked at the back of Edie's neck. One day she'd leave them, after they'd been so kind to her.

"You are thinking about those you left behind, are you not?" Songs Sparrow searching gaze studied Edie while still picking blueberries.

There was no use lying. Edie nodded. She toyed with the sprig she held.

"You are here for a reason. Sometimes leaving family is hard, but what you discover makes up for the loss."

Goodness, was Song Sparrow also saying Edie belonged here, besides Thunder Bear, Woman of the Sky, and Walks with a Limp?

"Yes, leaving is hard. My first year away from . . ." Edie couldn't say university. "Away from home when I went to the white man's school, I almost left I was so lonely for my family."

"But you stayed, did you not?" Song Sparrow ceased picking and rested the basket on her slim hip.

"Yes. I-I did. My mother . . ." Edie wet her lips. "She told me . . ." There were all kinds of ways to communicate, such as her cell phone, Messenger, video chat, and so forth. Being stuck in the wilderness of the eighteenth century made any form of communication impossible. "They do not know where I am. They will worry."

Everyone was probably worried when she didn't show up for the party. Mom had no doubt called the cops. Edie had probably made the news. Wait, she was native. Any woman with red skin was stored in the *who cares* filing cabinet.

"Trust Creator." Song Sparrow had resumed picking. "If you are here for a reason, *Gitche Manidoo* has foreseen any problems that may occur and has already addressed them."

Maybe Creator had? The faith of her people was astounding. "Your belief is strong."

"Of course it is. Why do you think we celebrate the *Midewiwin*?"

Edie almost dropped her container of blueberries. Back at her home reserve, they also celebrated the Grand Medicine, but seeing such a ceremony in its purest form before any influence by the Europeans was astounding. "Really?"

"We will be leaving soon."

"What about the crops?"

The twinkle in Song Sparrow's dark eyes was that of saying *silly girl.* "They are fine. The Great Mother will care for them. I will show you when we return how well-kept our crops are."

"Yes . . ." Edie nodded while swatting away a black fly buzzing around her head. "I wish to see."

Edie paddled back with Song Sparrow. The older women had urged the two to travel together so they could speak more. Along the way, they stole blueberries from the containers, then quenched their thirst by simply cupping their hands in the lake to sip. The refreshing liquid was so pure, filtration wasn't necessary, since Western society had not fully penetrated Lake of the Woods, ruining the water supply.

But the Europeans were here . . . somewhere, exploring and building forts for the fur trade Edie had studied in class.

"Where is the *Midewiwin* held?" Edie ran her wet fingers along her lips, licking the last of the water. She rode in the stern, proud to show she knew how to steer the sleek water vessel because Shoomis had taught her.

"*Gojijiing. Gojiji-zaaga'igan.*"

Song Sparrow had said *at the inlet,* then *Inlet Lake.* She was speaking about Rainy Lake, where the Rainy River emptied. The Point. Where Fort St. Pierre was built.

"Is there a fort there?"

Song Sparrow glanced over her shoulder and nodded. "Yes. It is where one of the trades happen."

The year must be around the seventeen hundred and thirties or forties if the fort remained in use. Pierre Gaultier de Varennes, sieur de La Vérendrye and his expedition could be here, or maybe up farther north on Lake of the Woods. Perhaps they'd already established Fort St. Charles. Maybe the French explorers had already left for Winnipeg. They could even be back in Montreal.

Also happening in this time period was the butchery of the Ojibway and their Cree brothers, along with La Vérendrye's expedition at *Massacre Island*. Edie's suspicions were correct. This was the beginning of the Ojibway and Dakota battles to claim this region that would last until the eighteen fifties, when her People would finally defeat the Dakota once and for all and call this place the home of the *Anishinaabeg*.

Where she'd grown up was rich in the names of battles and such. Sioux Lookout where they had watched for the enemy. Sioux Narrows, a town where combat between the Ojibway and Dakota had taken place. Warroad in the USA, aptly named because it was the place where the Ojibway met the Dakota to do battle.

The scarecrow had transported her to a time of war, which could end in doom for her, for Thunder Bear, or for both of them.

Chapter Six: Go West

Edie dipped her paddle into the river. The scent of summer was everywhere—in the spruce lining the shoreline, lingering on the water, and rustling in the light breeze to keep the heat of July at bay. She rode up at the bow of the birch bark canoe. Woman of the Sky commanded the stern and steered.

They were on their way to celebrate the *Midewiwin* at what Edie knew as The Point on Rainy Lake. Without the massive dam built by the town of Fort Frances controlling Rainy River and Rainy Lake, the water was untamed territory, unleashing its power over them, so much different than what she experienced in present day while out on the water with Shoomis.

When they eventually reached the rapids, they'd have to portage the canoes, instead of using the modern-day boat landing. This was the stopover where they'd settle for the night with another group of Ojibway, possibly the very location of Edie's home reserve.

Along the way, they'd passed two busy settlements of Ojibway who were readying to leave and join them on their adventure. Maybe those places were Long Sault and Hungry Hall, former Indian Reserves by Treaty that the Canadian government had dissolved in order to acquire the fertile land for farming, forcing the People to integrate with the other reserves, Shoomis and Koko had told Edie.

During her studies, she'd also read two to five thousand gathered for The Grand Medicine.

Preparation had taken some time for their journey to Rainy

Lake. They'd had to remove the birch bark coverings on the wigwam to use for their skeleton lodge at the ceremony site, then pack everything into the canoe. Their essentials weighted down the birch bark boat.

Edie had also gone with Song Sparrow to check on the garden, which had been as she'd studied. Instead of using today's Western farming's approach, the plants were placed in small mounds. This allowed the soil to hold and not be washed away by the rain. Complementary crops packed in the ground also protected the plants against bad weather and insects. Weeds were used around the garden's outer edges to further deter pests. While they were gone, the gardens were safe, which allowed her people to maintain their nomadic lifestyle.

Song Sparrow paddled beside them in the other canoe while her mother steered.

Walks with a Limp and Thunder Bear were in the scout canoes that rode up front and at the rear, keeping the women and children in the middle.

Edie kept glancing at the thick bush stretching along both sides of the river. The Dakota could be hiding somewhere. Moving camps was a vulnerable time, and the men were on the lookout.

In her car and depending on traffic, the jaunt from the mouth of Lake of the Woods to The Point was over an hour's drive. The trip from leaving their camp, traveling to the mouth of the lake, and entering the river was cramping her arms because they were moving west to east, not with the natural flow of east to west. Furthermore, she'd never paddled this hard while accompanying her dad or Shoomis on a leisurely outing, or for this long.

Sweat poured down Edie's back, soaked her hairline, drenched the bends of her arms and knees, and seeped between her legs. Even beneath her breasts the perspiration didn't stop. From the looks of the other women steaming ahead by submerging their paddles into the water with graceful yet powerful strokes, she was the only one suffering. Her strokes were becoming crooked, weak jabs. For a whole day she'd paddle, not stopping until they reached the rapids to make camp.

Her exhausted arms and lack of stamina, compared to the other maidens, would shame her. Maybe even bring shame to Woman of the Sky and Walks with a Limp. How many times had she read in non-fiction and fiction titles that the only women who belonged out here were those born for this land? She wasn't. She was a woman with red skin captured in the world of the white man.

The longer Edie fought to propel them forward, the feebler her efforts became. Finally, her aching arms could only stab the paddle into the water, which got them nowhere. Song Sparrow and her mother were way up ahead now. Edie and Woman of the Sky were falling far behind, far enough that they were now with the scout canoes.

The sun was merciless, burning its fierce rays of heat down on Edie. She'd smothered herself in bear grease upon rising, but her sweat was washing away what protected her skin from the UV rays and insects.

"Easy," Woman of the Sky called out. "You are not letting the paddle do your work. You are working the paddle."

Funny, Shoomis would've said the same thing. Edie removed the paddle from the river and rested it across her lap. She leaned over and cupped water to her mouth. Quenching her thirst wasn't enough, though. Her body cried to be doused in the cold liquid.

"Let me help you."

Edie hung her head. For Woman of the Sky to take the bow would be even more shameful. The older women always steered while the younger women did the hard paddling.

"I will be fine, but thank you for offering." Edie dipped her paddle back in the water.

Thunder Bear sat in the bow of the other canoe.

Walks with a Limp steered.

"What is going on?" Thunder Bear didn't shout but had raised his voice enough to be heard.

How could Edie admit she was tired and needed a break already? "My arm cramped. I will be fine."

He stopped paddling and tilted his head. Curiosity reflected in his gaze. Their canoes bumped. Water lapped at the freeboards. He laid his hand on both gunwales to keep them from separating. "Paddling upriver is a strenuous task."

Edie stared straight ahead, nodding. Murmurs came from the sterns. Maybe Walks with a Limp and Woman of the Sky were speaking about what a big failure Edie was. She couldn't help it. If she had to choose, she'd rather drive her car to the ceremony site. The white world was too ingrained in her to be like her ancestors.

"Look at me, Fire Woman." Thunder Bear's tone was coaxing.

She turned her head.

Concern lurked in his gaze. "If you are tired, say so. We can stop."

Edie raised her chin. "The others are not stopping."

"No, they are not, but they have lived this way their whole lives. You have not, have you?"

Running her broken nails — no longer a perfect manicure — along the paddle across her thighs, Edie nodded.

"I understand you wish to prove yourself, but people will have more respect for you if you work at your pace. No one expects you to master our ways even by the end of the summer."

"I . . ." Fine, she'd speak her fears. "I don't know if I can do this."

"I know you can. You were born for this. Now rest. Drink some water. Eat some jerky. Woman of the Sky will hold the canoe so the current does not take us back to where we came."

"I will," she dutifully replied.

"When we arrive, many will be proud you made the journey, no matter how long it takes us," he assured her.

Five days. A journey made by many in two full days. At the site of the camp, the shame wrapping Edie in its cocoon flew away on the breeze. Wigwams stretching far and wide were assembled on the spot that was cleared in present day. When they'd paddled down the river and into the mouth of Rainy Lake, there was no train bridge joining Canada with the United States. The boundary waters were still untouched by the imaginary line both governments had drawn down the river and lake.

The shoreline was also different, peppered with a sand bar and a huge beach stretching all the way to the reserve she knew in present day. Sans the dam built by the town, the water was not flooding the land.

The Cree would be here, and the Monsoni, who, at the time, were an extension of her People.

She gasped and covered her mouth at the imagery she had once only conjured in her mind that was now as real as the sweat running down her back. Fort St. Pierre stood tall, smothered by the massive four log walls carved into sharp points at the top. There were two bastions, one to the southwest and the other to the northeast. The main gate was closed, but men stood above on the sentry gallery, watching them paddle in.

Women and children either washed or played in the water. A game of lacrosse was happening. People had gathered to watch. Their cheers each time a favorite team scored carried to the canoe.

Edie couldn't spy the grand medicine lodge, but it was here somewhere.

The closer they paddled in, the more women and children surrounded them. Song Sparrow was one of them. She set her hands on the bow. "You did good." Pride reflected in her smile.

"Thank you. I need to bathe." Edie set aside her paddle. She never wanted to see one of these again. Fine, she couldn't truly complain. Viewing the Rainy River without the spoils of present-day towns and settlements had been a breathtaking experience.

Several women and children set their hands on the gunwales of the canoe and brought them to the shore.

"I will help you unpack." Song Sparrow assisted Edie from the vessel.

Edie needed all the help offered. Her legs and arms threatened to give out as Song Sparrow led her through the water.

"Again, thank you." If not for Thunder Bear's encouraging words, and Woman of the Sky's songs of strength, Edie would have simply fallen into the water and sunk from sheer exhaustion.

On wobbly, stiff legs, she was guided along the sand. She couldn't even stand straight because her muscles had locked, so she limped her way to wherever Song Sparrow led her. Laughter came from the children, and some from the women.

If Edie kept hanging her head, they might remain here, because it'd be buried in the sand like an ostrich.

"Keep your chin up. I have told many about you." Song Sparrow kept guiding Edie through the throngs of people. "They are aware you were raised among the whites. What you accomplished requires a feast. I will make something special tonight for you and your family."

"My family?" Edie squinted, then winced. The pain from sitting and paddling was enormous. She still couldn't stand straight.

"Yes. Walks with a Limp and Woman of the Sky. They treat you as a daughter."

"Oh . . . I am their guest." Edie had to quickly correct her. Nobody had mentioned anything about her being a daughter. She already had parents.

"I know. But they lost their daughter last spring. You are here now, living at their lodge. Woman of the Sky is training you as she would a daughter. You know this is our way."

A weird sensation of being watched spooked Edie like a ghost hovering around her. She almost stopped but kept hobbling along as she glanced toward the fort. The men remained up on the sentry gallery, staring at them. One in particular, dressed in tanned hide clothing decorated with fringes draping his firm body, zeroed in on her. His eyes, greener than the summer grass, almost seemed to pierce her insides. His brown hair was tied off his diamond-shaped face that possessed a coating of stubble.

Song Sparrow followed Edie's gaze. "They are our friends."

Edie nodded. She'd read how the French had befriended the Ojibway, even going so far as to learn the language. "Wh-why are they staring at us?"

"Maybe one is interested in marriage." Song Sparrow sassily chuckled. "It would not be the first marriage between a white man and a maiden."

Edie shuddered. Marriage *à la façon du pays* or *according to the custom of the country* — something she'd also studied. From the mixing of blood between the two races, this was how the *Métis* were created. Once these men had retired from the fur trade or sought a different line of work, they'd returned to Montreal or their home country. The majority had left behind the women and children they'd sired, thinking if the marriage wasn't valid in the eyes of the Church, they could freely abandon their loved ones, who'd devoted themselves to these men, for a proper *wife* that society and the Church approved of.

This was where the flame had sparked the out-of-control fire that the missing and murdered Indigenous women and girls had become in Edie's century — native women being nothing more than third-class citizens, savages to be used for sex. If a *good enough* white lady was not present, why not use a native woman?

Edie's eyes burned, and so did her chest. The pain engulfing her muscles vanished. She walked straighter, prouder. As an *Anishinaabe-kwe*, she'd look down her nose at these Frenchmen. Even Thunder Bear was slightly wary of their presence, although his People had befriended them. Maybe his vision had foreseen what would one day become of the Ojibway.

When the time came for Fire Woman to bathe, Thunder Bear would follow. The Frenchmen on the sentry gallery at the fort had openly admired the new maiden who'd arrived, but most were respectful enough not to gawk, except for one man in particular. Charlot Baudelaire. Handsome and with a flair for words sweeter than maple syrup, the Frenchman had cajoled his way into many a young maiden's fur robes while visiting the Ojibway camps.

There wasn't a chance Thunder Bear would allow the suave man near Fire Woman. Charlot even spoke the language, boasting proudly his father had been taught by the Ojibway of *Bawating*, the gathering place.

While Thunder Bear caught up with old friends, he kept his gaze positioned where Fire Woman and Woman of the Sky prepared the wigwam and unpacked their belongings. By the time they finished, the sun sat low. They retrieved their bathing essentials and made their way to the beach.

Thunder Bear followed. He glanced over his shoulder. The men had dispersed, all but Charlot Baudelaire, who was no doubt admiring Fire Woman's confident, sultry gait—something only a married woman possessed. With the basket on her hip, her chin held high, shoulders back, and legs gliding one over the other that produced a sensual wiggle to her buttocks outlined by the doeskin, sleeveless dress, she was a sight to behold.

Many a brave from different camps also cast her admiring glances. One approached.

"Who is this?" Defends the Arrow fell in step with Thunder Bear. "I could not help notice she came in late. Is she a new daughter for Woman of the Sky?"

"Perhaps." Pride swelled in Thunder Bear's chest.

"She is your . . ." Amusement lurked in Defends the Arrow's lingering question.

"We have shared many a walk."

"I see the white man with the greedy eyes cannot stop staring at her."

Thunder Bear would not give away his wariness of Charlot Baudelaire. No brave allowed another to see weakness in him. "Every man enjoys the sight of a pretty maiden."

"He is aware of our customs and no doubt is aware you have laid claim to her." The same amusement flecked Defends the Arrow's words. "What does Walks with a Limp say?"

"He understands I am courting her."

"She is older than the other maidens."

"That she is. She comes from a place far away where there is a white settlement. She was raised there and is learning our ways."

"Ah, that is why she is older than the others. Many have asked. Some even thought her to be a widow."

"No. She is as pure as the first snow, of this I am sure."

"When you have time, come and join us. We are playing

56

the moccasin game."

"I will gamble later. For now, I must see to Fire Woman's safety."

"That is her name? Wisely chosen. She is as stunning as the flickering flames . . . but her beauty could easily burn a man." Defends the Arrow snickered and swaggered off.

Thunder Bear's friend was correct. Fire Woman was capable of burning any brave with her beauty and the courageous spirit she had shown by the tasks she'd undertaken. Her determinedness in accomplishing the trek from *Pikwedina Sagainan* to *Gojijiing* proved her resilience, for she could have given up. But she hadn't.

She would make a fine wife. His wife.

CHAPTER SEVEN: PREMONITION NOW

The celebration was underway. Although Edie would not participate, she could spectate from afar at the spiritual event of the Grand Medicine Society.

Just by the way the *Midiwiig* decorated their faces, Edie knew which degree they held. For those of the first degree, the men and women had painted a broad band of green across the forehead. Narrow stripes of vermilion were decorated across their faces and below their eyes.

Those of the second degree possessed a narrow stripe also of vermilion across their temples, eyelids, and the region between their eyebrows. Just a smidgen above, a similar stripe of green was painted, then another of vermilion. Above the vermilion was again another stripe of green.

As for the third degree, they had red and white spots painted all over their faces.

The fourth degree used two different forms of paints. They either decorated their faces with vermilion, and a green stripe moving diagonally across it from the upper part of the left temple to the lower part of the right cheek. Or they painted their faces red, with two short, horizontal parallel bars of green across their foreheads.

Seeing her very own People this way took away Edie's breath. No amount of schooling could replace bearing witness to the Ojibway she'd studied in their true form and environment.

In preparation for the ceremony, the *Midiwiig* undertook a sweat bath just as the sun had begun to rise.

Edie hurried to the water to clean the bowls from the morning meal. She made her way through the throngs of people. Some had stayed awake all night, regaling friends they hadn't seen since last summer by singing and dancing their tales around fires.

"Good morning. I know most of the people but I have not met you yet." The greeting belonged to a heavily accented man who spoke Ojibway.

Edie stopped. She turned her head. Every muscle tightened. He was the man who'd stood on the fort's sentry gallery yesterday.

There was a swagger to his gait as he approached. He'd taken a razor to the stubble she'd previously witnessed to present a smooth, tanned face. "Charlot Baudelaire at your service. Allow me to help."

To ignore his offer was considered rude. Edie held out the bowls. Although it gagged her to say so, she did. "This is women's work. The men will—"

"But I am not *Saulter*." Charlot took the bowls. He continued to the beach.

Edie had no choice but to follow. She wasn't taken aback by his reference of *Saulter* either, for that was what the French had called the Ojibway who resided in this region.

"You are from France?" She almost threw her hand over her mouth at the mistake. She wasn't supposed to know countries.

Charlot quirked a lean, mink-colored eyebrow. "You are the maiden who lived with the whites, are you not?"

"H-how did you know?" She'd only arrived yesterday.

"Talk does happen. People visit other camps. Voices carry. They carried here. I would say you received quite the inquisitive welcome when you arrived yesterday." He stopped where the waves lapped at the wet sand, and crouched.

"Really, you do know I must perform this task." No man

in the camp would offer to help clean bowls.

"As you said, I am French. How I wish to conduct myself is my affair, is it not?" His green eyes twinkled. He immersed the bowl in the water. "Someone must clean up on our expeditions. We do not have the luxury of women accompanying us to aid in cleaning chores." He used a light coating of sand to scrub the bowl.

Edie squatted beside him. She grasped another bowl.

Still offering her a rich, wide smile, he sprinkled wet sand in her bowl.

"*Meegwetch.*"

"*Je vous en prie.*"

"I do not speak French."

"You understood, did you not?" He scrubbed another bowl. The light breeze brushed at his shoulder-length hair the color of the sand where strands had escaped from his ponytail.

"We should not speak." Edie rinsed the bowl. She set the birchbark container aside. "I do not think it is proper."

"Many maidens speak to us. How do you think we marry?" Teasing was in his silky voice.

"Yes, I understand." Irritation was an itch to Edie's skin. She couldn't help herself. Indigenous women of the twenty-first century still suffered because of the mindset begun in this century. When the rare man in her time was caught killing one of her own, he was given a manslaughter charge instead of murder for ending the life of her *Anishinaabe* sisters.

"And what will happen to these women once you leave the area?" Her words came out harsher than expected.

He blinked and stopped washing. His studying gaze searched her face. "One cannot take a woman of the forest from her home. She would never embrace the life of the white world if she were not born for it. To do so would tear out her heart. She would miss this." His hand swept the air, indicating the water, the trees, the shoreline, and the land across the way where the little town of Rainer had yet to exist.

"Really? That is your excuse for abandonment?" The question was hot enough to sting Edie's tongue that now resembled a hissing snake.

"We do not abandon. We aid as best we can. I am helping you, where your men view this chore with disdain. An affront to their honor."

Edie almost spat out, *I have studied your historical accounts of us in school. You bash our men without fully comprehending our way of life, and the role each person in the community is responsible for so we can flourish.*

Instead, she squared her shoulders and said, "We have our way of living. Do not pity us for the amount of work we do. Our role is as vital as the men. They would not have clothing if we did not prepare the hides they bring us. Nor food if we did not cook what they have hunted. We are equal in all respects."

"They take wives, you do not take husbands."

Edie had to stop her laughter because she had studied accounts of women who had taken two husbands. But she could not elaborate or she would have to speak about the book she'd read by a female ethnologist who'd interviewed many native women at the turn of the nineteenth century. "Maybe we do, but your men who write about us have not taken the time to ask."

Charlot's eyes widened.

In order to hide her smirk, Edie ducked her head to look as if she was concentrating on what she cleaned. "A word of advice. Do not look upon us through how you live. Look at us as how we live."

"You have lived with white people. Why come here then?" Curiosity was in his question.

"Women also must seek their vision when they are young. My vision told me I must come here," Edie lied.

"Where did you come from?"

A lump of fear filled Edie's throat. "I . . . I cannot say, for if I do, people will know who my family is." Hopefully, he'd buy her second lie.

"I see. So . . . you have lived in both worlds. If myself or one of my associates offered marriage, we could take you with us once we returned." He set aside the last bowl.

Edie gathered up the six she'd brought. "I have no intention of marrying. I am here to learn. Nothing more."

"Every woman seeks marriage." Charlot's answer was smug and confident. "How would she survive without a man to aid her?"

"There are many widows in your world who survive on their own, do they not?" Goodness, the arrogance of men in this time period. Edie stood.

"They do, but it is a difficult life for them." Charlot offered a weak smile. "My intention is not to offend. I simply hoped to ask if you would like to take a walk when your chores are finished."

"You know I cannot walk alone with you." Edie pivoted and moved along the sand.

"Bring a friend. I would be most delighted to entertain you both."

"I came for the Grand Medicine. But thank you for asking." Edie quickened her step. People were staring. That didn't look good. She dashed behind a wigwam before Charlot could catch up.

She ran straight into Thunder Bear. His sturdy chest almost crushed the bowls she held.

"And where are you rushing to?" Amusement was in his tone and dancing eyes. He took the bowls she held. "Come. I will help you return them. I thought we could walk."

Charlot had been wrong. Here was Thunder Bear taking Edie's bowls she had to pack away.

Thunder Bear glanced beyond her shoulder. His eyes narrowed. She followed his hostile gaze to Charlot, who had followed her. He stood for a moment, nodded at Thunder Bear, then turned on his heel.

"What did he want?" There was a growl to Thunder Bear's question.

"He helped me wash the meal bowls. Nothing more." Edie started walking.

Thunder Bear cleared this throat.

Edie pivoted. "Yes?" She'd assumed he'd follow.

He blinked.

What? She was supposed to let him lead? Okay, the eighteenth century was getting on her last nerve. "Join me. I am going to the lodge."

He smiled. Apparently, her answer had appeased him. He fell in step beside her, still holding the bowls. There were some amused looks cast their way. Maybe the men didn't assist with women's chores and found helping beneath them, which meant Charlot hadn't lied.

"What did the Frenchman want?" Thunder Bear stared straight ahead.

Edie folded her hands in front of her. "As I said, he offered to help. Nothing more."

"Be careful. I do not trust them." There was ice to his warning.

"I thought your people had befriended them?" Edie skirted around a few people. Already the camp was wide awake. Some were eating. Others had resumed a few games.

"They are not *my* people. They are *our* people." The terseness in his reply was a true reprimand.

He was right, too. She was *Anishinaabe-kwe*. "Correct."

"They did befriend them, but I am wary. What is wrong with these?" He held up the bowls.

"Nothing. They are more than satisfactory."

"So why do our people trade for the white man's materials?" His face remained masked, but emotion continued to carry in his voice.

Edie understood he would not shame himself by showing his anger. He was a warrior and must maintain his composure.

"Do you wish for the tin, baubles, and cloth the white man offers?" There was questioning to his voice.

Of course Edie missed her cell phone, mattress, central air, shoes, and car. She'd spent the last five days paddling the Rainy River. Although she appreciated the so-called mixture of ashes from the fire pit made into a paste to wash her hair, and the bear grease to smooth her long locks, she'd kill for her favorite brand of shampoo and conditioner. She'd also kill for a real toothbrush, toothpaste, and dental floss, instead of what Woman of the Sky had offered.

"Your silence says everything," he said, more to himself.

Edie stiffened. She was being selfish. Woman of the Sky didn't have to make the bristle-like brush and paste she used to cleanse her teeth. At the lake earlier, when she'd first bathed, some women had chuckled while watching Edie scrub her mouth. They'd been even more amused when she'd used the fine twine of deer hide to floss her teeth. She'd almost read their thoughts — *brushes are for hair*. That was another thing. She was reduced to using a piece of wood with porcupine needles attached to tame her locks.

"More silence, I see," Thunder Bear murmured. "Understand this, Fire Woman." He stopped at the wigwam. His features were as stoic as always.

She gazed up at him.

He lifted his hand. His fingers grazed her chin.

She held her breath. Couples or those who were sweet on each other never touched each other in public. The print of his finger was pure heat on her skin, too.

"I am courting you." The seriousness in his statement was strong hands grabbing her by the shoulders and hauling Edie to her tiptoes.

Any second, she expected his mouth to ravage hers. All she could do was stare because her muscles had gone into shock.

"In due time, you will not desire the possessions of the white man." There was triumph mixed with finality in his speech.

She wet her lips. "I come from the white man's world."

"You may, but you are destined for here, otherwise you would not have walked through the flames. Is this not so?" More triumph smattered his speech.

Edie drew back her shoulders and stared him square in the eye. "What you say is true, but it does not mean that I do not miss what I once had."

"Then why have you not returned to the flames?" His slim lips edged up at the corners.

"Maybe I wish to see more before I return?" She lifted her chin.

"Return?" There was no fear in his eyes, or shock. His mouth kept curling. "You will not return, for you know you are destined to be with me. With us." He gestured at the people. "It is why you persevered and made the trip here, although we kept asking if you required help. You are determined to prove you belong here. And I must say, you make me proud. For one so slight, you are strong and courageous."

His compliment was silk sliding along her bare arms, even lips pecking the nape of her neck. She couldn't stop the shuddering of her spine or the quivering between her legs. Something ached in her groin. A flutter. As if he'd slid his finger . . .

She gasped. He'd made her experience arousal.

More triumph lit in his dark eyes. "Put away the bowls. I will wait." He released his finger from beneath her chin where it had remained during their conversation.

Edie gathered the bowls from the crook in his free arm and ducked inside the wigwam to Woman of the Sky refreshing the bedding.

The older woman smiled. "Such flush skin," she murmured. "Do I dare ask if Thunder Bear accompanies you? He stopped by earlier. I told him you went to the lake to wash the bowls."

"I . . . I . . ." Edie set the containers in their proper spot.

"What is it?" The warmth from Woman of the Sky's silent approach was on Edie's backside.

Edie turned her head to Woman of the Sky on her haunches, a breath away. "I am beginning to question myself."

Woman of the Sky brushed at Edie's loose tail snaking over her shoulder. "Do not be afraid. This is why we celebrate The Grand Medicine. It is a time of renewal. Do you not think the People were afraid when the sacred *miigis* directed us to move where the food grows on water? This is why we must celebrate, for we found our true homeland—where *Gitche Manidoo* willed us to be."

Edie was well versed in the studies of the Ojibway's migration from the east to where they resided now. "But the Sioux already occupied this land."

"They are not destined to be here." Woman of the Sky shook her head.

"There is much war." So much war, Edie had studied how during this time period, the fur trade had suffered because the Ojibway and Dakota had been too busy fighting one another. A battle was stirring, ready to explode again. History had foretold this.

"Please do not concern yourself with the business of men. Remember, we all have our place in the community. This is what we must concern ourselves with." Using her finger, Woman of the Sky drew a circle to indicate the wigwam. "You still have much to learn. Now, forget your fears and go for your walk. He waits."

Edie nodded. She rose and left the wigwam.

Chapter Eight: Ceremony

Edie sat legs to the side as all women did, while Thunder Bear sat cross-legged. They could not access the huge, long lodge with the curved ceiling, swathed in birch bark. Already, many people had gathered inside.

The sun was almost high. Not a cloud peppered the view of pure blue.

The drumming and singing banged deep in Edie's chest. She closed her eyes and let her body sway to the sacred song. Each beat was the pounding of the Great Mother's heart. Each wail was the singing of the wind.

For the ceremony, she'd braided her hair and donned the beautiful dress Woman of the Sky had helped Edie make as her first project on sewing deer hide, although she'd yet to learn how to skin one and tan it into clothing. That would come with time.

A porcupine necklace was fastened around her neck. Porcupine quill earrings with pretty stones were looped through the lobes of her ears. She'd taken paint to her face, drawing red lines along her cheekbones, yellow across her forehead, and orange on her chin to proudly state she was a woman of fire.

Thunder Bear was done up just as regally in a fringed buckskin shirt that hugged his proud chest and honed arms. Fringes ran along the sides of his leggings. Beautiful beadwork of black, green, and white decorated the tops of his moccasins. The black of course represented his spirit animal, the bear, and the green was the forest where the creature dwelled.

As for the white, that was the thunder pounding in the sky.

Edie knew how much the *miigis* shells meant to the People. In her studies, archeologists had proved they could only be found far east in North America where the Ojibway had originally resided at the Great Salt Water Lake. Told in one of the *aadzookaang*, the sacred narratives, was the *Midewiwin*, and the promised long life by practicing the teachings.

"Cease thinking as a white man." Thunder Bear's gentle order was steamy on Edie's ear. "Think as *Anishinaabe-kwe*."

He was right. She was forever referring back to her studies when she should be allowing the ceremony to capture her spirit. Just like everyone else here, she sought the good life, free from sickness, starvation, and enemies. If only she could sit inside the *Midewiwin* Lodge and see firsthand the ceremony in its purest form. There would not be any new initiates into the society. Woman of the Sky had informed Edie that only took place during the spring, not late summer.

The lodge had been constructed farther from the fort to keep away prying eyes. Only the *Anishinaabeg* were present, and their Cree and Monsoni cousins.

The ceremony lasted well into the evening with prayers, songs, and readings from the sacred birch bark scrolls.

Edie stood to begin the meal for Walks with a Limp and Woman of the Sky, who remained at the ceremonial site. She glanced back over her shoulder at the lodge she'd studied about in her classes. Her home reserve had a grand medicine lodge, but nothing close to the size of the one here.

A few other maidens also returned to their wigwams to begin feeding their families, leaving the older women to continue to witness the ceremony.

She strolled around one of the many domed lodges and almost slammed into Charlot. He held out his arm to steady her.

"You are in such a rush." His warm fingers held her elbow. "I am to assume you must now serve your family food."

"Yes." Edie inched backward. His gaze almost seemed to scrape her bare skin as he studied her.

"Tell me, do you believe?" He fell in step beside her.

Edie glanced at him since he walked her pace while puffing on his pipe. "Believe what?"

"In what you are witnessing?"

"Why would I not?"

"You have lived with the English. Surely, they schooled you in their religion."

"No, they have not." Which wasn't a lie, because she'd grown up learning everything about the traditions of her people through her grandparents. "You do not believe?"

Charlot chortled. "No. They are merely superstitions, nothing more."

"But you told me you would marry a maiden."

"*Oui.* Still, I have no intention of converting. Some do, though."

Edie understood many voyageurs had lived with her People, while just as many chose not to. Charlot was of the latter, she assumed. But she doubted he was a voyageur. She was assuming him to be a *coureur de bois.* "Why do this?" The grass was comfortable beneath her moccasin feet.

"Why do what?" He puffed on his pipe.

Being the evening, many from the fort had probably wandered outside to enjoy a smoke and a light walk before retiring. The scent of roasting fish drifted under her nose. They also must be cooking.

"Leave your motherland. Live here. Trade here."

"I was born here. My father was the one who said goodbye to France and took passage on the ship."

Edie stopped walking.

Charlot's green eyes were brighter than the grass in the morning with dew upon it. "Why are you here? You do not covet the powder, ball, axes, knives, chisels, and awls as your men do from us."

"I told you why I came."

"And if you should return east?" The sun sat lower. The light rested on his face and hair, bathing him in golden brown. "Will you seek passage?"

Of course he assumed she was from the east, since that was where the white settlements were. "I will not return east." Which wasn't a lie because she'd instead go through the flames.

"A pity, for I would have offered you passage." His smile was slightly crooked, like a naughty boy.

"Yes, at a price, I presume." She stopped at her wigwam. "I must ready the meal."

"I will help . . . if you do not mind."

"Cooking a meal for those who welcomed me into their lodge is an honor. To show my gratitude for their generosity, I must do this alone."

"Then I shall keep you company. I expect you will not cook in there?" He pointed at the wigwam.

"Of course not. I will cook the meal outside. First, I must ready the fire."

"That, I shall do. You go ahead and ready what you require to make the meal," Charlot suggested.

There was no point in arguing. Plus, Charlot did not seem as dubious as when she'd first spied him on the sentry gallery at the fort. She did understand he was attracted to her. As handsome as he was, the feeling was not mutual. Could he be a friend, though? An ally? Perhaps. He did respect the work she did.

Still, she could not look at her chores from the view of a woman of the twenty-first century. False pride and the need for constant praise was abhorred by her people. Doing one's duty was simply that — attending to chores and nothing more. She must keep remembering to view herself as one of the

People, and the importance of her contribution allowed the *Anishinaabeg* to flourish. Therefore, praise and appreciation were not required, as was in her century, for she already knew her worth to Woman of the Sky, Walks with a Limp, Thunder Bear, and the rest of the camp.

Only once the fire had burned down and was simmering coals did she lay the wrapped fish for cooking. She also wrapped some vegetables, wild mushrooms, and onions she'd picked with the other maidens who'd generously helped her to decipher what to choose for eating.

Charlot returned, holding a tin cup and his pipe. He sat.

"You are not eating in the fort?" Edie sat with her feet tucked beneath her thighs.

"No." He shook his head.

The hint was apparent. To not offer was rude. "You helped me with the fire while I readied everything. You are more than welcome to join us."

"*Merci.*" He raised his cup toward her. "I accept. I look forward to sampling your cooking."

"There are others who are much better cooks than I."

"You are far too modest. Did you not cook when you lived in the white settlement?"

"Yes, but it was different."

"I can imagine. Is this your first time cooking over a fire?"

"I have cooked over fires before . . ." With Shoomis and her dad when they'd take her fishing for walleye and she'd prepare the shore lunch. "Each time I hope I am improving." Because she'd always used a cast-iron frying pan in the past, available lard, canned potatoes to slice, and other twenty-first century essentials.

She glanced around. Woman of the Sky and Walks with a Limp were nowhere in sight.

A few maidens at their own wigwams, cooking their meals, glanced in Edie's direction. Their admiring stares were not cast at her but Charlot.

"How many summers have you seen?" she asked.

"Twenty-six. And you?"

"Nineteen."

He hiked a brow. "You did truly grow up in a white settlement. Normally, you'd be married by now."

Heat gathered on Edie's cheeks. "Yes, I have been told."

"I am not attempting to insult you. Not at all. You do not strike me as a woman who would accept the first offer."

True. Plus, marriage was simple among her people. If Thunder Bear came to her lodge in the middle of the night, and she accepted him, and he stayed until morning, Woman of the Sky and Walks with a Limp would welcome him as her husband. Thunder Bear would remain in their lodge for a full year, providing for her family, while she made the essentials they required to begin living in their own lodge.

More heat gathered on her face. She had forgotten such intimacies happened with others present, albeit the amorous couple were hidden under robes and had their own space in the wigwam, as she did now. The odd night she'd cover her ears when hearing the low moans and soft whispers coming from Walks with a Limp and Woman of the Sky's side of the wigwam.

No doubt British and French women shared the same dilemma, for many lived in simple one-room houses to keep the heat contained during cold winter nights, so this predicament wasn't exclusive to the Indigenous people.

"You are always quiet. There is much for you to take in, is there not?" Charlot puffed on the pipe. Smoke billowed from the bowl.

"Yes, there is." Frustration gnawed at Edie. She came close to throwing up her hands. Maybe she should return to the portal once they arrived back at Lake of the Woods. As wonderful as this was to experience her People in their true environment, there was too much to digest, plus, she missed her friends and family.

Thunder Bear had said not to worry, that *Gitche Manidoo* was overseeing Edie's journey.

True, she couldn't deny the beauty of being here, of experiencing this place in time before the almost-destruction of the People had occurred. But the ripple had begun. Even Thunder Bear, as much as he was wary of the French, owned a gun, powder, and balls. He took arms against the Dakota and would do so again until they were forced out of this land.

Walks with a Limp and Woman of the Sky emerged from around a wigwam.

Edie's heart sank a smidgen because Thunder Bear did not accompany them.

"My stomach led me here." Walks with a Limp smiled and sat. "Charlot. Welcome. I was wondering where you have been. I saw you when we arrived and meant to offer you greetings."

"I took it upon myself to come seek you out. Fire Woman has been keeping me company," Charlot replied.

Woman of the Sky glanced at Edie. "You have cooked, so I will serve. Relax."

"*Meegwetch.*" Edie grabbed a rush mat and took the only place available, which was beside Charlot, to eat her meal.

While the men talked about the upcoming trapping that occurred through the late fall and winter, Edie searched the crowd of people flowing through the maze of wigwams, but there was still no sign of Thunder Bear. He must be eating with his family.

She almost chided herself for getting her hopes up. Although he admitted to courting her, the crazy dilemma of returning home clung to Edie like a second skin—part of her wanting to stay and experience the way of life she'd dreamed about from an early age, but the other tugging for her parents and grandparents.

The meal had yet to be served, so she stood and politely excused herself. She wove her way around the lodges.

A *jaasakiid* stalked in her direction. His searching stare penetrated the paint circling his eyes and drawn down his face in bold lines.

Edie couldn't help glancing behind her, but her gut said he had stopped for her.

"Come." The *jaasakiid* curled his finger. He turned and strode toward the ceremony site.

Edie followed. Curiosity raced through her veins, matching the quickening flow of her blood. The *jaasakiijig* belonged to the *Midewiwin,* but were seers of the *jiisakii,* shaking tent, where they sought the *manidoog* for answers to their questions.

They arrived at the site where only a few people remained. A few spoke to the remaining *Mideg* present.

The *jaasakiid,* maybe in his forties, sat on a tree stump. He motioned at the other stump. Edie joined him.

He held an eagle feather. "I saw you coming." As he spoke, he moved the feather around. "I was a child at the time."

Edie was aware *jaasakiijig* began having visions as children and later studied under older *jaasakiijig.*

"I saw big birds in the sky carrying people and the belongings of the white man." His eyes had rolled back into his head. He kept waving the feather around.

The wind rustled.

Edie rubbed her bare arms. She assumed he was referring to airplanes.

"People lived in trees that almost touched the clouds."

Skyscrapers.

"Moose pulling people and goods along lines that were straight or curved."

She almost slapped her hand over her mouth because

trains did not exist in this time yet. He had seen the twenty-first century.

"Canoes moving at great speeds."

Oh geez, he foresaw boats and motors.

"More canoes stacked one on top of the other."

He'd even seen cruise ships.

"The Great Mother spun faster."

So true, everyone raced through their day in her time period, never stopping to appreciate the gift of life the Ojibway sought through the *Midewiwin*.

"The People were forced to turn away from all we taught them."

Edie's heart cracked. He was referring to the Indian Residential Schools.

" . . . forced to live in one place."

And he'd also seen the Indian Reserves.

"But they never truly forgot." His eyes stopped rolling. He stared through the paint circling his eyes. "You never forgot." He thrust the eagle feather. "You wished to live with us and learn our true way, and you will, but you must take it back to them."

"Wh-what?" Edie's mouth fell open. Was he saying she'd return to the twenty-first century? Yes, she'd assumed so. Returning home was constantly in her mind. Now that he was confirming the truth, fear gripped her in its talons.

She did not want to return. Her heart ached for the People, and most of all Thunder Bear. Gosh, while talking to Charlot, she'd been mulling over her family. Now her spirit had spoken loud and clear of what she truly desired.

Thunder Bear sat cross-legged at the lake where the moonlight shone over the water, casting a silver glow to the light waves. Every *Midewiwin* ceremony was his time to reflect on his vision quest, no matter how much his heart ached to join Fire Woman at her wigwam to eat the meal she was serving, and where the Frenchman was present, attempting to woo her.

The man in Thunder Bear demanded he rise from his place and take what was rightfully his. But the warrior inside him said to continue courting her as a true *Anishinaabe* brave should, that she wouldn't fall for the sweet nothings, sly smiles, or white man's presents Charlot would offer her.

In the past, Thunder Bear had never lost faith she would arrive, and now she was here. He closed his eyes to visualize the nest his father had made for him at twelve summers, where he'd sat for six sunrises, listening to the tales from the Thunderbirds.

The mighty beings had spoken to him about the creation of Turtle Island, of the four-legged, winged, and finned creatures, and of the *Anishinaabeg*. They'd shown him the Great Salt Water Lake where the People had first lived, the migration of the Ojibway to the land where the food grew on water, and the enemy who waited for them that slithered on the ground and hissed with their snake tongues from the foliage, ready to wage war on the People to stop them from claiming the place that rightly belonged to the *Anishinaabeg*, for they were keepers of the *miigis*.

He had to join his fellow brothers-in-arms to continue to stake this land as *Anishinaabeg* territory and send the Sioux farther west and south where the Thunderbirds had instructed Thunder Bear the *Little Snakes* truly belonged.

After six sunrises, he'd assumed that was his true quest — ridding this area of the Sioux, which was why he hunted and trapped furs to accumulate as many arms from the French as possible. Not so. On the seventh sunrise, the Thunderbirds presented to him the red road he'd already been told to walk by his parents and grandparents — a road every true Ojibway journeyed. A crooked road full of curves and steep hills, the true path of life leading to the sacred spirit world where death no longer lurked.

He'd seen a woman way far ahead of him. While he walked upright, her footsteps were staggered, even lurching, and sometimes she fell and struggled to get up. The Thunderbirds had ordered him to retrieve her, to bring her back to where he walked, for she needed his help. He understood the request because every Ojibway embraced assistance, since helping each other was why the *Anishinaabeg* existed, and how they survived and flourished.

No matter how fast he ran on the red road, he could not reach the woman who remained far ahead, still stumbling and staggering.

The Thunderbirds had told him he'd never catch her, for she was at a place that was impossible for him to touch. They said they would help him. He was instructed to make the journey every summer from his camp to the place of the steep rocks, underbrush of buttercups, and vast spruce trees to wait for her. She would appear through flames so bright and beautiful that he'd wonder if he'd seen the spirit world. They commanded him to call her Fire Woman, for the woman on the road he could not aid would be as beautiful as the dancing flames with the courage and bravery of a warrior.

Now she was here, cooking a meal at her lodge and being wooed by the Frenchman. The most Thunder Bear could do was trust the Thunderbirds, for there had been more to his vision of her. Ensuring her survival was his first priority, the mighty beings had insisted.

CHAPTER NINE: DEEPLY ORDERED CHAOS

When the wild rice season — what the Ojibway referred to as the harvesting and processing of the *manomin* that grew on water — had arrived at the end of August, the camp had broken up into family units. The women had headed out in canoes with their sticks to knock the ripe kernels into the bottom of the vessels. In turn, the men had hunted ducks and geese. During September, the women had gathered the last of the chokecherries and earl cranberries for winter storage while also engaging in much fishing.

They were at their new camp now. They'd stay here until the time came to tap the maple trees during the Sugarbushing Moon. Being so close in proximity, and coming to care so much for these people who not only opened their home to her, but also their hearts, the words *mother* and *father* had rolled off of Edie's tongue one day while speaking to Woman of the Sky and Walks with a Limp. They in turn, baring proud smiles and love shining in their eyes, had referred to her as *daughter*. She'd never forget the way they'd embraced her, their hugs full of tender care and happiness.

Woman of the Sky's younger sister, husband, and children had joined them, along with her father, mother, grandmother, and grandfather.

The days were growing much shorter and the nights longer during the time of the Falling Leaves Moon, as Edie knew October to be. Thunder Bear's camp where he resided with his *dodem* was a hike to the lake plus a good paddle by canoe. Without him here to keep her company, Edie's real family kept surfacing in her mind. Her heart also ached for Song Sparrow.

Soon, Thunder Bear would leave to trap the beaver, muskrat, and mink to trade for more balls, powder, and guns in the war against the Dakota. Weapons were the only possessions he seemed to covet from the French.

She finished gathering the wood, a daily chore she was used to now. They mainly cooked indoors at the second fire. Their winter lodge was double insulated with additional birch bark coverings and moss. Instead of the domed shape of their spring and summer lodges, their winter home was a peaked roof and rectangular in length to accommodate the extended family.

Tightening the blanket around her shoulders, she trudged back to the wigwam.

"Why so sad, Granddaughter?" He Paddles on the Crooked River asked. He was Woman of the Sky's grandfather. Since there was no word for great-granddaughter in Ojibway, he always referred to Edie the same as he would Woman of the Sky.

"Do I look sad?" Edie squatted to set down the wood she'd collected. Her wool point blanket with the green, yellow, and indigo stripes fell, a gift from Charlot when she and her family had left the site of the *Midewiwin*. He'd told her women loved them and wore them as a coat during spring and fall, even winter.

She had to admit the blanket served its purpose, because a robe of thick fur would have been too warm to drape around herself.

He Paddles on the Crooked River nodded. "Do not worry. He is seeing to his family before he sets off. But he will come."

Edie ducked her head.

"Do not be shy," he chided. "I am told Puckers Her Lips had the same expression when we were young many moons ago and I was not present in her camp." He winked one wrinkled eye.

"I . . . I must go inside and finish some chores." Talking about her love life with her great-grandfather wasn't a conversation Edie wished to engage in, even if the old man meant well.

She darted into the wigwam to Woman of the Sky working on the nettings for fishing. "I smoked many yesterday. Did you need me to catch more?"

"No. I am checking, that is all. Making sure there are no weaknesses in the nets." Woman of the Sky kept studying the nets while she spoke.

Edie stirred up the cooking fire. The smoke billowed through the opening in the top. She'd learned much from her new mother, new auntie, and best friend. The constant chores and forever being outside had done one trick — Edie slept better. Every night, no matter if home or Thunder Bear plagued her mind, she was so tired, falling into dreamland came easy.

The same for her body. Even though she'd always been fit, her arms and legs were honed from constantly paddling a canoe or walking, spearing, or netting fish, picking berries or herbs, harvesting the garden, and knocking wild rice . . . The work was endless.

There was always something to repair or mend. Soon Walks with a Limp, and his brother-in-law, Swift Deer, would leave to hunt, since the deer and elk were fattening up for the winter. Hunting wasn't done during the spring and summer months, not when fish were plentiful.

Edie had sampled and learned how to cook every kind of fish, from trout and whitefish to sturgeon and walleye. Woman of the Sky had also taught Edie the essential parts of the fish. Bones were used for needles and stock in soup. Eyes were a delicacy.

Her new diet left her already slim figure super trim. No matter where she poked, not an ounce of fat covered her flesh.

Did she still crave a bag of chips or pizza? The odd moment she did, but not as often as before.

Obsessing over the time had also slowly left her. She no longer missed her phone to check what the clock read. Now, she operated as her ancestors by embracing the light of day for her routine of morning, high noon, afternoon, and evening.

"Ah, I was speaking about you," He Paddles on the Crooked River cried out, his leathered voice carrying into the lodge.

Edie froze. Thunder Bear? She quickly checked her braids that had loosened from the hard work she'd performed today. Her face wasn't scrubbed, either. She glanced at her dress and smoothed the doeskin material.

A light laugh came from Woman of the Sky.

"Puckers Her Lips and I said we missed seeing you, and here you are."

Edie froze. Great-Grandmother hadn't been present when Great-Grandfather had talked about Thunder Bear.

"*Bonjour, mon ami,*" Charlot called back. "It is good to see you, too."

Edie was aware French traders visited the Ojibway camps, but she hadn't expected Charlot to stop in. Maybe he was on his way to Fort St. Charles.

"You are in time for the meal. My granddaughter is cooking us the sturgeon she caught this morning."

Star Dancer, Woman of the Sky's sister, prepared the meal for them this evening at the cooking fire.

"Offer him some tea. The water is heating." Woman of the Sky shoved her chin in the direction where the kettle hung.

"I will." Edie grabbed three tin cups and fixed the spruce

tea. One for herself, one for Great-Grandfather, and one for Charlot. She flavored them with the ration of honey. Borrowing the sweet delicacy from the bees had been an interesting chore. The black-and-yellow creatures had to be smoked out first to harvest the golden nectar they produced, which was then stored in birch bark containers.

Edie slipped from the wigwam.

Using a long stick, Charlot poked at the outside fire. A capote that fell to his knees draped his taut body. The hood was at rest. A wool cap, or toque as she knew them to be in her day, covered his light-brown hair.

He Paddles on the Crooked River held out his hands. "Thank you, Granddaughter." He always had a *th*-sound to his speech because of his missing teeth.

"It is good seeing you again, Fire Woman." Charlot gave a slight nod of his head.

"It is good seeing you, too." She offered up the tea.

Charlot grasped the tin mug. For a moment, his fingers clamped around hers. The heat from his skin was tiny shocks of electricity shooting from Edie's palms to her toes. Quickly, she stepped back. Having moved too fast, she stumbled slightly, and almost fell on her rush mat. The tea in her cup jostled. Thankfully, none spilled over.

"Granddaughter, what has you behaving so clumsily?" There was teasing to He Paddles on the Crooked River's chiding. Even amusement.

Heat from embarrassment settled on Edie's cheeks. She sat with her legs to the side, rewrapped the blanket around her, and clutched the tin mug close to her chest.

"What have you brought this time?" Great-Grandfather asked, seeming to forget his earlier jesting. His black beady eyes had settled on Charlot.

Although Charlot gazed at Great-Grandfather, he stole a peek at Edie, then returned his attention to the old man.

"News. Sightings of the Sioux from Fort St. Pierre. They remain on the other side of the lake, though."

Edie drew in a sharp breath.

He Paddles on the Crooked River rubbed his chin. "If you know this, then they know this." He slurped his tea.

They meant the other Ojibway living in the area on Rainy River and Rainy Lake. From what Charlot had said, the Dakota were sticking to the so-called USA side of Rainy Lake and Rainy River. Hearing they were in the area, and not having Thunder Bear nearby, was fear stretching its arms around Edie.

She hadn't come here to get killed by the Dakota. She was also a good hike and a paddle away from the portal to escape danger.

He Paddles on the Crooked River continued to sip his tea. At his age, of course he was nonchalant about the news. Probably because he didn't have anything to lose, having lived a long, full life.

Swift Deer, Star Dancer's husband, approached the fire.

Great-Grandfather held up his hand to Charlot, most likely indicating he stay quiet for now. Maybe the old man was worried about the news he'd received.

"My friend, this time of the year is rare when you visit." Swift Deer's brows furrowed. He sat beside Great-Grandfather.

"I am on my way to Fort St. Charles. I thought to stop in, visit my *Saulter* companions, and be on my way in the morning." Charlot held his cup up in a *cheers* sort of manner.

"Where are your supplies?" Brows still knitted, Swift Deer glanced around where Charlot sat.

"With my canoe." Charlot tipped the cup very high, most likely polishing off the last of the tea.

"Fire Woman, be a kind host and help Charlot retrieve his belongings," Swift Deer ordered. "Then make him up a bed of furs."

Edie stood. By now she was used to the commands coming from the men. The liberated, twenty-first century woman inside her had stopped balking and accepted she wasn't being ordered about like a servant, but simply being tasked to perform a chore, one of respect for their guest.

Charlot rose. He took them to the worn path that traveled to the lake. Edie followed behind. Within the thick bush — nobody ever called it the forest or woods in modern day because of how dense the area was in foliage and trees — she treaded lightly over the fallen leaves.

He also treaded lightly. A man of the outdoors, as crafty and cunning as his Ojibway friends, he'd been trapping from the age of twelve, from what Edie had been told.

She gazed up. The sun was setting. The trees cast shadows everywhere, some that could perhaps belong to the Dakota. "Do you think they'll come this way?"

"Why would they not?" Charlot's reply was one of detachment and acceptance. "This has been their home for ages."

"Do you think this war will go on for a long time?" She ducked a stray branch in front of the path. Why she'd asked was beyond her, because she already knew the answer from her studies in school.

"It will not stop until your people have what they want. The *Mideg* are convinced this is their true homeland. Did they not say as much at the *Midewiwin*? You witnessed what they spoke about."

Strange, this was what the settlers in the US during the nineteenth century had also believed. They'd been convinced *Manifest Destiny* was pointing them to conquer the land of the West and shape it into what lay in the East. To bring the old-world ideology into the new. The Democrats had been adamant about taming the west, but numerous Americans, even Abraham Lincoln, had rejected the idea.

"What is it, *ma chérie*?"

Edie almost stopped walking. Wasn't the French term an endearment?

A light chuckle came from Charlot. "If I was courting you, I would say *mon amour*. Please do not be offended. We are friends, are we not?"

"Yes." She cleared her throat. "If your family is back east, why trap? Why not stay there?"

He gave a throaty chuckle. "I was born for this. It is in my blood. I will not stop, just like my father, until my bones protest from age."

"Is that why your father stopped?" The scent of moss and spruce was everywhere.

"Yes." He kept leading them along the path. "Out here, there is peace. Is this not why you came here? For the peace? For the virginal land as pure as a maiden?"

The word *virgin* dusted heat along Edie's cheeks. "Yes."

"We were born to do what we do, but like me, you will eventually return to your people, will you not?"

The moisture left Edie's throat. Thunder Bear flashed in front of her eyes. "I do not know."

"Ah, you hesitated before answering me." Charlot wagged a finger but kept walking. "You know as much as you love this land, your destiny lies elsewhere once your time has come to bid *adieu* to the home of the *Saulters*."

"That is what you will do? Bid *adieu*?"

"*Oui*. For me to remain out here means death when I am too old to fend for myself. I will have to return to civilization as my father did. Why do you think your people live in bands? And in the summer live as a village? To fend for yourself out here alone means death. Even the wolves know so. They form packs, do they not?"

"You seem to have adopted our teachings."

"When my people first sailed over, they had to learn how

to live with the land, and your people taught us how. Many do remain. Once you experience this paradise, it is hard to leave."

"You will leave . . . with regret then?"

"My father left with regret." Charlot almost seemed to sigh. "When I was twelve, that is when he took me with him. I am his only son. I have two older sisters. They are married and have families of their own."

"You mentioned he taught you Ojibway."

"*Oui.* As I said, he learned from the People of the Falls. My first season here, I was terrified, but by the second season, I could not wait to come back."

"You went home to visit family?"

"For the summer. Out here, fall and winter are my time to trap the land for furs. And trade them. By spring, the rivers and lakes have unthawed, and that was when I would paddle home."

"When were you last home?"

"It has been five years."

So that was why he'd been at the fort during the summer. He probably stayed there, or replenished his supplies.

"Why work independently instead of for a company?"

The sound he made resembled a scoffing snort. "My father was a *coureur de bois*, and I honor his tradition. We spit on the *congé* system. I do not need a license to trade or New France telling me what I can and cannot do. My father established many wonderful relationships with your people and introduced me to many."

"Yet, he went back to Montreal."

"As I said, he has my mother to care for. If not, he would have . . ." Charlot came to a sharp stop. "We are almost there."

Edie knew what he'd prevented himself from saying—his father would have married an Indigenous woman, joined her family, and never would have returned to Montreal, because she had a good hunch Charlot's father was born for this. He probably even missed the interior greatly. Maybe this father had been in a love affair with a maiden and had produced offspring he'd never see.

CHAPTER TEN: WILD HEARTED SON

Edie set the last of Charlot's packs beside the wigwam. Everyone had already gathered around the fire—eating, talking, joking, some burping. Since Star Dancer was in the midst of savoring the meal she'd cooked, Edie bent at the fire to retrieve a serving of fish and some wild rice cooked in maple sugar and dried berries for Charlot to feast on. She held out the tin plate to him.

"*Merci, ma chérie.*"

She dipped her head slightly, as all maidens did, and fixed her own dinner. The corner of her eye caught the amusement in Swift Deer's gaze and the knowing glances between Star Dancer and Woman of the Sky.

Gnashing her teeth, Edie plopped down and picked at the sturgeon. Even cooked with delicious herbs, the scent of the fish wasn't appealing to her souring stomach because the women had taken notice of Charlot's amorous interest.

He'd brought them more plates and cups, which Edie's meal and water were served in. She was aware from her studies that the *coureur des bois* had first traded European goods for fur with her people, then eventually became trappers, besides traders. By the time of this century, Charlot was of the latter. He was Catholic, no doubt, and had probably been schooled by the Jesuits back east.

They continued to eat while small talk was made. Edie finished the last of her food.

"Now for my true gift." Charlot set aside his cup and plate. Curiosity simmered in the eyes of the family.

89

Noise of wood popping and snapping came from the cooking fire, since the warming fire consisted of heated stones. After sitting in the cooking fire to heat up, the stones were brought over to the warming fire using two pieces of deer antler.

"I thought you could use these." Charlot spread out three more point blankets. "Keep your toes nice and cozy, hmm?"

The delight in Woman of the Sky's eyes said she appreciated the gifts. "*Meegwetch.*"

"*Je vous en prie,*" Charlot replied. He opened his capote. A red belt was cinched around his lean waist. Attached to the belt was a cup for his pipe, tinderbox, and tobacco.

Edie gathered up the gifts. They would be evenly distributed among the women. The appreciation directed at Charlot from the others soothed away the earlier stress tightening her muscles, for he did truly understand this country, knowing giving was more respected than what a person accumulated.

Once Edie finished her task, she returned to the warming fire, keeping the blanket wrapped tightly around her shoulders. The wool easily trapped her natural body heat within the cocoon.

Charlot had lit his pipe and puffed.

Swift Deer and his family had retired to their designated spots at the back of the large wigwam. So had the grandmothers and He Paddles on the Crooked River. That left Kicking Elk, Woman of the Sky, and Walks with a Limp.

Edie sat between her mother and grandfather.

"Why don't you stay and visit," Woman of the Sky suggested. "I will tend to the chores of cleaning."

Something resembling an icicle spread across Edie's gut. She glanced at her mother. "What do you mean?"

Rising, Woman of the Sky cast her a knowing smile. She bent and whispered into Edie's ear, "Never make it easy for a man. Thunder Bear is courting you. Let him earn you, daughter. Enjoy Charlot's company." With a soft giggle, she gathered up the bowls and disappeared from the wigwam.

Mortification steeped in Edie's chest. Her very own mother was telling her to play both men against each other? Perhaps this was what Woman of the Sky had done in her youth when Walks with a Limp had courted her.

There was a smile her father tried to hide by the way he folded his lip over the other. He glanced at Charlot. "Where did you come from?"

Their conversation was lost to Edie whose thoughts wouldn't cease. Were her parents hoping Charlot would try sneak into her sleeping robes tonight? Well, if he attempted to, his greeting would be a slap, no matter his pride. She was a twenty-first century woman, and she allowed no man to attempt his seduction on her. She'd move her bed of robes to where her parents slept, and he'd then get the idea to keep his hands to himself.

Edie couldn't stop shifting on her bed of robes. Facing the wall of the wigwam indicated to not disturb a person while they slept, but trying to stay on her one side had cramped her arm, since she always bedded down on her opposite side. Her parents were at her feet. Their deep breaths said they were far away in dreamland.

Charlot was awake. From the sounds of logs being placed in the fire, and the snaps and hisses as each one caught the flames, he was tending to their main resource for warmth, just as Walks with a Limps or Swift Deer did each night.

She could almost feel the Frenchman's eyes on her backside, his green gems burrowing deep into her flesh. The scent of his pipe mixed with the sweet aroma of burning wood.

His turned-up nose at his own government by refusing to purchase a license for trade said how reckless and rebellious he was. A man who made his own rules. She couldn't see him settling with a maiden, and he'd admitted to bedding a few.

The familiar ache that had hounded Edie between the legs after meeting Thunder Bear resurfaced. Charlot wasn't responsible for the light throb. Only one man could extinguish the longing heat. Edie cupped her breast. Why keep torturing herself? She should call it a day and leave.

Without Thunder Bear's presence, her heart continued to ache for her parents, brothers, and sister. Her friends. The people she'd met at university. Yes, she loved living among her people, and she'd learned so much, but she'd only stayed this long for one man. The words the *jaasakiid* had spoken clawed at her mind.

"You are thinking about home?" The words were whispered.

Edie stiffened. She rolled over. The fragrance coming from her bed of rabbit furs was heaven to her nose. The softness gliding along her skin was a luxury not even the most expensive bedsheets could produce. There wasn't a chance in hell she could leave all this behind.

"Is that why you're tending the fire?" She did her best to keep her voice low.

"Come. I boiled some water. I made fresh tea. Join me." Charlot's invitation wasn't one of seduction, but of a lonely man who could use some company.

Beneath the robes, Edie wiggled into her dress. She'd taken a shine to her parents' philosophy and doffed her clothing before sleeping, the best way to get some rest. The deep breaths coming from Woman of the Sky and Walks with a Limp said the quiet chatter hadn't disturbed them. Only soft snores came from the back.

Edie slid from the robes. She grabbed her moccasins and tiptoed to the fire.

Charlot stood. He motioned at the wigwam entrance.

Edie gathered the wool blanket around her shoulders and

followed him outside to a black sky full of shimmering stars.

"Winter Maker approaches." He pointed to the constellation Edie knew as Orion.

"Yes, he does." She stood beside him and took the tin of tea he handed over. "For some reason, I always get . . . maybe excited when I see it. My parents' house faces the south. When I lived at home, I always went out on the porch to look at it."

"The winter sky fascinates you?" He held out his tea.

"Yes. More so than the summer sky."

He unhitched his cup from his red belt and began readying his pipe. "When were you born?"

Edie almost gasped. The middle of January. "The . . . winter."

Charlot cracked a smile. "You are a winter baby. Of course you appreciate when *Biboon* arrives. Out here," he extended his hand, " . . . it is not the same as back east. *Biboon's* reign of terror is brutal, yet he is generous. He gives me my livelihood during his wake time."

"I understand winter is harsh out here." Edie tilted the mug and sipped.

"You will not know it until you experience it." Charlot seemed to say the words to himself.

"Do you know of anyone who turned *wiindigo*?"

"Oh yes, my father told me a few stories. Some had to be put out of their misery, for they only desired human flesh."

Edie couldn't help her sharp intake of breath. Those people had been killed. She had to remember the law of the twenty-first century didn't exist here. "They could not be helped?"

"You know as I do, it is rare a person can escape once a *wiindigo* consumes them. Death is true mercy for them."

Edie shuddered. Hopefully, no *wiindigoog* appeared this winter. Her twenty-first century self said she was being silly, but having her feet planted in the eighteenth century said otherwise about what modern-day people likened to as folklore.

"Have no fear. I will protect you," Charlot reassuringly said.

"Did you ever have to eat bark?" She used her finger to stroke the tin mug.

Charlot nodded. "When I was fifteen. It was a harsh winter. Very harsh. The water was high that year, and it drowned the wild rice. Game was scarce. My father was boiling the fringes from his coat and softening the bark to make our dinner . . . edible." His gaze took on weariness, as if recalling the horrible nightmare. "When you are that hungry, you understand why people turn *wiindigo*."

An icy shiver claimed Edie's spine, almost freezing her stiff.

"Your mind no longer works. Your muscles ache beyond any form of relief. Your thirst cannot be sated. You are delirious. You cannot even sleep. If not for my father, who knows what would have happened to us. He hauled me on his back and found a settlement where your people were. They . . . saved us."

He turned to her. "Understand, I have nothing but respect for your people. They taught us how to survive out here. We would not be doing what we are doing if not for our *Saulter* friends."

He puffed on his pipe. "Not even that merciless winter could stop me from living out here. I love this land and the people."

"You sound as if you will regret returning as your father did."

Charlot's rose-colored lips sank downward. "I think I will. Maybe I will find a place to build a small home out here . . . if the right woman comes along." The thoughtfulness in his gaze vanished, and he cast her a sly glance.

Edie hugged the blanket tighter around her.

"Your parents do not disapprove. If they did, they would

have asked me to bunk down beside your great-grandparents."

"Wh-what?" Edie almost dropped the cup.

"As I said, many marry your women." His eyes crinkled.

Edie stepped back. "I am being courted by Thunder Bear."

"So you are . . ." His quirked brow said he didn't give a darn. "But I do not see him here."

"You know he has obligations. He hunts the ducks and geese for his family before he leaves to trap." Edie thrust her chin out.

"As do I have obligations. However, I did make it a point to visit you, did I not?" His French accent became more pronounced, as if he wanted to tell her sweet somethings in his native tongue that he couldn't articulate in *Anishinaabemowin*.

"Y-yes, you-you did." She tightened her fingers around the cup.

"Perhaps you will allow me to steal a kiss, then?" Delight richened the green in his irises.

"As I said, Thunder Bear is courting me." Edie took a step back. "I should retire. I am sleepy. Goodnight, Charlot."

"Sleep well, *ma chérie*." He gave her a tiny salute but continued to smile.

Thunder Bear lay under his robes. For four days he'd been on the hunt, sitting in the reeds of the lake during the night, luring ducks to him using his decoys and duck calls. Although his tired muscles begged for sleep, rest never came because his mind kept wandering.

Acting too hastily might fluster Fire Woman. She was still growing accustomed to their way of life. He had to control the lust consuming his groin. Visiting one of the accommodating maidens he had in the past or enjoying the company of his father's Sioux slave was a definite no. To bed down with another woman was an insult to what his heart felt for Fire Woman.

His vision and the Thunderbirds had told him he'd marry Fire Woman, but the waiting was testing his warrior patience. Taking her as his wife and teaching her everything about her People had been imperative, the Thunderbirds had insisted. So was ensuring they had children.

Then there was the burning ache in his gut during his quest, followed by flying with the Thunderbirds high in the sky, so high he could almost touch Winter Maker twinkling above the People in the charcoal-colored sky. What this meant he did not know, for nothing had been revealed to him.

He did see a barren place of long grass, though, a place he was sure he'd one day experience in the flesh.

His arms lay stretched above him. It was best not to dwell, for when the Thunderbirds felt he was ready to learn more, they would reveal to him what the puzzle meant.

He slipped his hand inside his bed of robes and cupped his swollen flesh that hardened whenever he thought about his most cherished gift from the Thunderbirds. Tomorrow, he would paddle to Fire Woman's camp. The freezing-over moon was upon them, the lake getting colder, and the odd sprinkling of snow drifted over the land.

He caressed himself and used his thumb to spread the arousal coming from the tip over his length for easier strok-ing. Her sensual thighs were before his eyes, a kissable spot that led a seductive path to where he yearned to fill her wet, pink flesh. He could almost taste the hairs covering her mound, and the scent left from a day of chores that produced the lingering aroma of womanly perspiration.

He stifled the moan aching to leave his throat. Her breasts hidden beneath her dress taunted him. What color was the skin encircling her nipples? Maybe a dark brown? He could almost taste them. The swollen hardness he jerked back and forth was becoming an unbearable ripple on the lake ready to explode into a storm and swamp him.

He could only imagine what he'd feel being deep inside Fire Woman, pumping between her slim legs. Her tightness. Wetness. The heat her snug flesh would produce wrapping firmly around his erection.

The pleasure was building. He stroked himself quicker. The excitement jolted through him like the shimmering lights of the thunderbirds crackling during a storm. He had to hold his hand over his mouth to keep from gasping aloud.

He couldn't take this anymore.

Tomorrow, she would become his wife.

Chapter Eleven: Edie, Ciao Baby

Thunder Bear steered the canoe to the bed of rocks on the shoreline to the path that led up to Walks with a Limps' camp. Father Sun was hiding this morning. Gray clouds smothered the sky. A mixture of rain and snow speckled his face. Another canoe was present. The construction of the structure told him the water vessel belonged to the Frenchman, Charlot Baudelaire.

A smidgen of annoyance gathered in Thunder Bear's chest. Yes, another in pursuit of a maiden was only natural, just as their feathered and four-legged teachers of the male persuasion had to compete with their rivals to win the right to mate. A woman expected the best suitor to take her hand, just as she had to prove herself worthy as a wife by excelling in all chores related to the gentler sex.

The Frenchman was well aware that until Fire Woman became Thunder Bear's wife, Charlot could continue to attempt to court her.

Thunder Bear made his way to the camp. Leaves decorated the ground that was readying for a long sleep. Soon, the lake would freeze. Wherever Charlot was trapping this season, he'd best get moving before *Biboon* appeared with his cold breath of frozen air.

When Thunder Bear came through the last of the trees, he arrived at a camp in full work-mode. His eyes lit. Fire Woman sat before the outside fire filleting fish. The children played in the leaves by tossing them up in the air and watching them cascade down over them.

"Welcome. Welcome." He Paddles on the Crooked River raised his tin cup. "Come. Join me."

"Where are the rest of the men?" Thunder Bear stole a peek at Fire Woman who stared at him beneath her lashes as she continued to cut the fish.

"Are you seeking someone in particular?" The wrinkles around He Paddles on the Crooked River's eyes became more pronounced to match his curled, wrinkled mouth.

"Yes, I am. I wish to speak to Walks with a Limp."

The old man's thin lips broadened into a full grin. "Is it the Frenchman's company that has brought you here?"

"I was not aware of his visit. I just saw his canoe upon my arrival." Thunder Bear squatted. He rested his hands on his thighs. "Where is he?"

"With Swift Deer. They shall be back soon. The others are in the lodge." The old man slurped his tea. "Stomachs always make decisions for hungry men." He motioned at Fire Woman. "As for Walks with a Limp, he went to answer the call of nature. He shall return soon."

Thunder Bear nodded. He stood. Fire Woman kept her head ducked, but the odd tilt now and then said she was stealing peeks his way.

His ego plumped. He strutted over to the fire. "What are you making for the morning meal? You are truly mastering your chores."

By the light in her dark eyes, Fire Woman was pleased by his compliment. "Fish. I'm going to cook it the way I did for my father and brothers. A bit of bear grease and some seasoning." She also had cut up wild mushrooms. A bowl of dried berries nested beside them.

"I can hardly wait to try what you are serving." He stood. Acknowledging her presence and paying her a compliment was his way of telling her she'd been in his thoughts. Now he must leave and let her finish her work, since she was busy feeding the family.

"Thank you," she murmured.

Just then, Walks with a Limp came from the bushes.

"Please, serve us some tea," Thunder Bear gently ordered. It was time to speak to a man who he'd one day call his relation. He strode up to Walks with a Limp. "It is good to see you again."

"How are you, my friend?" Walks with a Limp made his way to the fire.

"I hoped to see you before I leave." Thunder Bear fell in step. "I need to speak to you."

"Yes, the animals have donned their winter fur. We will miss you." Walks with a Limp smiled. "My brother-in-law will leave soon, too." He held out his hands and accepted the tin cup Fire Woman offered.

Thunder Bear thanked her for the tea she handed him.

Without a word or a glimpse at them, Fire Woman strode back to the fire.

"Swift Deer is readying to depart." Walks with a Limp let out a breath and stared at his leg he'd almost lost to a cougar ten winters ago. He still wore the animal's fur during the winter moons.

"You must miss accompanying him." Thunder Bear sipped the maple-sugar-laden tea.

"This is my life now." Using his hand, Walks with a Limp made a sweeping motion. "It is best not to dwell on yesterday and what one cannot change."

Wise words. Thunder Bear nodded. "What of the Frenchman?"

"He leaves after we eat."

All able men were readying to head out and trap the animals for their precious fur. "You know my intentions regarding your daughter."

A smirk formed on Walks with a Limps' lips. "I thought

you would speak about this." His gaze wandered to the bush. "Seeing as who our visitor is . . ."

Thunder Bear cast away the grimace wanting to form his mouth into a crooked scowl, refusing to shame himself by displaying a hint of jealousy. "He is an able man. A handsome man. But . . . he is not me." He quirked his brow.

Mentor or no mentor, friend or no friend, Thunder Bear knew Walks with a Limp's loyalties lie on ensuring the best man won the hand of his new daughter. "He may bring gifts, but he does not possess her heart."

"You are that man?" Amusement reflected in Walks with a Limp's eyes, although his tone was serious.

"Yes, I am. She is still new to our ways. I ask a favor from you."

"What is that?"

"If you and your wife are in your usual sleeping spot, Fire Woman will be very uncomfortable if I come to her tonight . . ."

"It is our way. Something she will have to get used to." Walks with a Limp shrugged.

"Yes, I know, but as I said, she is still too new. She will be more comfortable if you are at the back of the lodge."

"I see . . ." Walks with a Limp set aside his tea and clasped his hands together. "You are asking for us to bed down beside my wife's parents for tonight?"

"Come the morning, when I leave, what I acquire in furs will belong to you and your family," Thunder Bear promised, meaning he would be their son-in-law and begin paying his debt to his new relations for one round of the seasons required of him.

Walks with a Limp pressed his lips together. His eyes traveled to a bare poplar tree. "Let me think. Before we retire for the day, you will have my answer."

Thunder Bear had expected no less. No man made quick

decisions. Patience was a virtue amongst his people.

Just then, the Frenchman and Swift Deer returned, carrying two partridges each. There had been no shots, so they must have caught the slow-witted creatures with their bare hands.

"Something for your evening meal." The Frenchman held up the birds.

Thunder Bear stole a peek at Fire Woman. She'd disappeared inside the wigwam, most likely to begin cooking the morning meal.

"*Meegwetch.*" It was Star Dancer who held out her palms for the birds. "Always so thoughtful, my friend."

"It is my pleasure." The Frenchman gave the birds to Star Dancer. He looked to Thunder Bear. "It is good seeing you."

"It is a pleasure to see you, too," Thunder Bear replied, and the warmness in his voice conveyed he did feel the same way.

Blue jays squawked from above, giving their *doink, doink* call. Some migrated, seeking the warmth of Winter Maker's brother *Niibin*, who resided in the south, while other jays chose to remain.

Thunder Bear gazed up at what was a sure sign. Just as the *diindiisiwag* of the forest built their nest together, reared their young as a team, and mated for life, so would he and Fire Woman. She would never walk away from their union, as was allowed. Ever.

Edie feasted on the partridge Charlot and Swift Deer had brought to the camp. Grease ran along her fingers as she continued to bite into the juicy breast. The sun was already sinking low behind the tree line. Night was coming too fast, and Thunder Bear still hadn't departed.

Not only did her belly sing with joy from the delicious treat, her heart skipped a few beats. Maybe they could spend some time together alone before Thunder Bear left. Perhaps this was why he'd come to their camp.

There'd been so many chores that had kept her busy ever since the summer, from the ricing season to drying berries. Much had to be done before winter arrived to ensure their bellies remained full during the cold season. She'd even learned how to make pemmican, the dried meat easy for storage and a quick meal for a harsh winter day if there was no fresh deer or elk to eat.

During her evening chores, Thunder Bear's gaze bore into Edie's backside, and her hands shook. The women took notice and giggled, too. She did her best to brush off the light teasing.

Once she was finished cleaning up, her heart seemed to grow bigger, readying to burst through her ribs because Thunder Bear had smoked a pipe with her father and retired to the lodge. How was she supposed to sleep with him lying in a bed of robes where Charlot had slept last night?

She glanced around at those who hadn't retired meandering to the lodge. Tightening the blanket around her shoulders, she dipped her head and shuffled through the opening of the wigwam to Thunder Bear feeding more wood to the burning cooking fire.

Edie's gaze zeroed in on the spot where she'd slept last night, safely at the heads of her parents. She wouldn't move her robes again. They'd stay put in their usual spot. To move them would insult Thunder Bear, since seeking the safety of her parents was a woman's way to deter a potential suitor. Yet, what if he came to her while Woman of the Sky and Walks with a Limp slept?

If she turned him away, he might mistake her fear for rejection. Somehow, she had to make him understand the commitment she'd be undertaking.

Wait, she was getting ahead of herself. He might simply want to spend the night before he left. Blood flooded her toes and fingers. She plopped down at the warming fire full of hot rocks and sat on a rush mat.

Thunder Bear kept stirring up the logs, poking and breaking up the wood to burn better.

"The seasons are true." Nothing like what Edie experienced in the twenty-first century. The November cold was a bone-chilling awakening to reality. Shoomis had spoken about the weather many times and the changes to Mother Earth from his childhood. He'd also mentioned in the even older days, snow could become thigh high. Minus twenty-five Celsius was the average temperature come winter.

"Of course they are." Thunder Bear set aside the stick. He moved from the cooking fire to the warming fire and also sat on a rush mat. The glowing rocks reflected in his dark eyes. "Why do you say so?"

Edie picked at a fringe on her dress. "We spoke about how I come from a place far ahead." She pointed. "The Great Mother grows warmer there."

"Warmer?" He squinted.

She nodded. "Yes. Terrible things are happening. She is being taken for granted."

Thunder Bear frowned. "To neglect or even abuse one's mother has a great impact on her children. They suffer when she suffers."

"There is much suffering." The butterflies that had sat in Edie's stomach all day vanished. Maybe his soothing timbre was molding her muscles into a slippery batter like heated bear grease.

She stole a peek at the back of the lodge, where Star Dancer readied her seven-year-old and nine-year-old children for sleep. Edie's great-grandparents were already under their robes. Grandmother was making up the bedding for Grandfather.

"Who is suffering?" Thunder Bear knitted his black brows.

"Our people." A shallow breath left Edie's mouth. "It is why I was educating myself in the white man's world."

"As long as we have this" — using his hand, Thunder Bear made a sweeping motion — "we will not suffer."

Edie would refrain from speaking about the reserves and how there wasn't enough land to hunt properly, harvest properly, or much less do anything properly to live as they lived now. How the sturgeon had almost vanished and were now being reintroduced through a program by her home reserve. How a dam had almost stolen the mighty rapids of Rainy River, and the vanishing of the massive sand bar on the south side of Rainy Lake.

She had the opportunity to remain here forever. Her heart didn't ache for what was missing, for they were nothing but material possessions that were hurting the Great Mother who groaned in protest. If she let Thunder Bear come to her tonight, she'd become his wife and never have to deal with the problems plaguing her century.

"Much thinking goes on here." Thunder Bear tapped the side of his head. "What is it, Fire Woman?"

"Part of me misses my family, and the other part wishes to never leave here," Edie murmured.

"Understandable. I wish I could take you with me when I leave to trap the furs, for this would ease your sadness for home, but you have much to do here while I am gone," he gently said. He moved his rush mat closer to hers.

His scent invaded her nostrils, as clean as the forest and purer than the water of Lake of the Woods with a touch of well-tanned leather, and the woodsy sweetness from the pipe he'd smoked earlier. There was nothing *fake* about him.

He was as natural as his namesake in the bush. No forged smells of cologne, scented shampoo, or fragranced soap. No unnatural haircut or hair color. No groomed eyebrows. No fashionable clothing. Yet he was handsomer than any male who posted his photos on social media. Nor would Thunder Bear engage in the online petty bickering that broke out between races over the latest news.

He was a doer, not a talker. Her ancestors were quiet people, who lightly laughed for a reason—because words could not be taken back once spoken. They compared menial chatter to the mindless squawking of the magpie.

"What are you thinking about?" He reached over. His fingers glided along her cheekbone.

Edie stole a peek at the back of the lodge. All was now quiet. Only the shadows of their sleeping forms of her relations could be seen. Her parents were absent from their usual spot. They, too, had retired to the back of the lodge.

Thunder Bear's potent gaze was as mesmerizing as the dance of the flames. She could almost taste the richness of his red lips, feel the ripple of his lean muscles that weren't over-pumped biceps bought at a gym but came from eating naturally and working and living outdoors.

He leaned in closer, stretching toward her. His fingers continued to caress her face. The breath left her lungs. When his mouth came down on hers, she claimed it with her own lips.

Chapter Twelve: Fire Woman

Edie couldn't get over the plushness of the kiss. Thunder Bear's soft, wet mouth was smothering her. He explored her lips with lush but gentle strokes.

For so long, apprehension had tapped at the back of her mind because she knew her time to choose was coming. She locked her arms around his strong shoulders and chose him.

His muscles tightened beneath her palms. She couldn't resist caressing his round delts that were firmer and harder than baseballs. This was the very reason why she'd never gotten serious in high school or university. She'd been waiting for Thunder Bear to be the first to truly touch her.

Yes, she'd been kissed, but nothing like the teasing suckles being lavished on her. His tongue eased between her lips, and she welcomed the silky heat penetrating her mouth.

A kink was growing in her neck, so she shuffled in closer until their knees brushed. The electric heat his skin generated crackled along her thighs and shot through her veins. His natural essence was intoxicating, mixed with the lovely scent of the fire.

His tongue was wet and hot, sweetly tasting hers. She couldn't get over the gentleness of such a strong man, or the succulent pleasure his licks were producing. Never was she so aware of the shivers rippling through her. To say waiting for the right man had been the best idea was a generous pat to her own back. Thank God she'd never listened to Mom or her friends.

Thunder Bear had said she'd been *born for this*. He was

right. Sure, she'd kill for a glass of milk and a real shower, but small sacrifices were nothing compared to the new life she'd been granted.

She could have let him kiss her forever. His tongue was showering hers with deep, drawn-out circles and light licks. There was the sweetest *hmm* sound buzzing in her ears.

His fingers feathered her waist, setting off her pulse points to become thundering gallops close to bursting. His strokes remained firm yet tender. He didn't move his hand anywhere else but simply explored her waist.

An ache was budding between Edie's thighs, the familiar want ever since she'd first laid eyes on Thunder Bear. Her body was demanding he take her. A trickle of fear seeped down her spine. If she let him claim her and stay in her robe of furs, he would become her husband.

Thunder Bear broke the kiss.

Edie's stomach dropped in disappointment.

He gazed into her eyes. His fingers touched her face. "You know what will happen?"

"I . . ." She wet her lips. "Y-yes." She nodded.

"Do not be afraid." Using soft strokes, he kept rubbing her face.

"I am not afraid of what is to happen, I am . . . I am unsure of what will happen afterward."

"You will be my wife, that is what will happen afterward." His declaration was quiet yet stern.

"I . . . I will never see my family again. Or my friends."

"You have family and friends here. *Gitche Manidoo* made sure of this, did he not?"

"Y-yes, he did."

"I will take good care of you, Fire Woman. I will never mistreat you or hurt you. This is my promise. You have my word." Honesty clung to his statement. "You have seen nineteen summers. You are more than ready."

"I-I missed you."

"And I missed you, too." The seriousness in his gaze liquified to tenderness. "I missed you very much. But we both have responsibilities. You know this. You are a brave and courageous woman. Do not let your fear interfere in what your destiny is."

"I . . . I will not." The shivers kept bumping along her spine.

"Then let me have you as my wife." His request wasn't a plea but a simple suggestion.

She didn't believe he'd ever beg or plead with anyone but *Gitche Manidoo*. The word rolled from her throat, "Yes."

His mouth came back down over hers, and she was sucked into the dreamy kiss he'd lavished on her moments ago. She eagerly met his tongue and laid gentle strokes on his silky flesh invading her mouth. His taste was pure nature. He was pure nature. Her thoughts faded away, and she enclosed her arms back around his strong shoulders.

He laid her back on the bed of robes she'd made for him earlier. The fur almost seemed to close in around her like a cocoon. The crackling and popping coming from the fire was all the romantic ambience she needed. Tucked away in the wigwam, she'd never felt so ready to be one with someone.

While he continued to lavish her with kisses, he snaked his hand up her thigh. His fingers glided back and forth. His skin on hers was a hot sensation reaching between her legs that demanded she spread them open to unearth what was next to come.

He joined her on the robes, laying his body over hers. His fingers continued to stroke her outer thigh. His maddening touch was creating a fire within her hotter than the one burning. The crazy ache between her legs kept intensifying. She almost begged to rub her thighs together to seek some relief.

His lips moved from her mouth and pecked her jawline.

"Touch me, Fire Woman," he murmured.

His quiet beseeching drained the oxygen from Edie's lungs. He, too, was suffering from the maddening fever erupting between them. Even wilder, he rose for a moment to remove his buckskin shirt. When he bared his solid chest and bronzed skin with the red undertones, her eyes almost popped from their sockets at the masculine essence he presented to her.

As he lay back over her, she set her hands on his pectoral muscles and met powerful firmness beneath his warm flesh that was softer than the doeskin she'd been tanning the other day. Even his rich scent was that of the four-legged creatures who meandered the bush.

She ran her hands along the wide space of his back where more muscles rippled beneath her fingers. His mouth was on her neck, drawing the skin between his teeth where he suckled. Steamy breaths from between his lips heated her ear. His hips were gyrating in the same rhythm as hers, and she hadn't even known until now she'd been grinding back and forth, even rising slightly to rub against his groin.

Something hard was pressing on her leg. Her heart almost jumped out of her chest. He was erect. *Oh Lord.* She came close to slapping her hand over her mouth, but the darn appendage was too busy gliding along his waist.

Nor could she pull her hand away even if she wanted to. This was the first time she'd ever gotten to explore a man this way. This was the only time she'd wanted to explore a man this way.

Age twenty-four in the eighteenth century was so different from the twenty-four-year-olds she knew in the twenty-first century. Thunder Bear possessed the wisdom and maturity of a man in his late thirties. Maybe this was what her heart had desired for so long—someone who saw the world through her eyes, instead of gaming, parties, hook-ups, and clubbing.

Perhaps this was why she'd never truly fit. Even though she had wonderful friends, she'd yet to meet someone who she connected with, and that person was here—now.

His hand was pushing her dress up. The soft fringes danced along her outer thigh. A groan came out of nowhere and escaped from her mouth. He was still lavishing her neck with suckling kisses, leaving a wet path to her ear.

Her dress continued to inch upward until the heat from the rocks warmed the ache between her legs, and a puff of air. She stiffened.

"Don't be afraid," he whispered. "What will happen is as genuine as nature itself. Do not let the teachings of the white world influence you."

He was right. There was nothing to fear. She buried her face in his mounds of thick hair. His heavy breaths were moistening her neck. The skirt of her dress was around her waist.

He shifted. The warmth cocooning her vanished. She lay on her back, gazing up at him. He stared back while he removed his breechclout and unfastened his leggings. His strong thighs and erection that stood proud and long were before her. Edie wet her lips. Yes, she'd stolen many peeks on the Internet of naked men, but nothing had prepared her for a flesh-and-blood man in the real raw. Curly black hair nested his groin. His balls were tight and full. He removed his moccasins and set them beside his clothing.

She sat up on her elbows, unable to peel her gaze away from his magnificent body of flat abs, sculpted chest, and strong shoulders. The bear claw necklace was the only item he did not remove.

He shifted to his knees and held out his hands. She moved off her elbows and took his fingers in hers. He gently kissed each of her knuckles while his mesmerizing gaze continued to burn into her. The soft pecks were heaven on her skin, his lips pure satin.

He released their entwined fingers and buried his hands into the hem of her dress. With her heart almost beating in her throat, she moved to her knees. He drew the garment upward. As he lifted the dress up and over her head without bothering to detach the sleeves, the soft doeskin caressed her skin.

She was naked before him, but shame or embarrassment did not claim her cheeks. Her throat had gone dry, and she ached for a cup of water. Thunder Bear's roaming gaze was touching her breasts, feathering her arms, stroking her stomach, and gliding along her thighs. The potency in his eyes was fondling her between the legs, exploring a spot no man had yet to penetrate.

His red lips moved into a pleased smile. "You are beautiful, Fire Woman. More beautiful than I could think or imagine."

"You . . . you imagined me naked?" she sputtered.

"Many, many times."

His sensual declaration was a tongue feasting between her thighs, licking and tasting. She clasped her hands together and shivered.

"Cold?" He quirked a brow.

"No." She shook her head.

"Liar." His reply was teasing. "Let me warm you up."

He gathered her into his arms and showered her with kisses that started out slow and gentle then twisted into firm and demanding. She fiercely licked back, claiming his tongue as her own. Everything about this moment felt so right. Her nerves were not shot but fluttering with excitement, burning with anticipation.

While still kissing her, he laid her back onto the bed of robes that claimed her skin with pure plushness. Her breasts were melted against his chest. His erection was pressing on her, and the seeping excitement sneaking from him was wetting her pubic hairs.

His hand captured her bottom, and she gasped. He rubbed

her ass, using soothing relaxing strokes. Every muscle she possessed unwound from her harried anticipation. She stretched her arms over her head to let him feast on her.

His mouth encircled her nipple. His tongue danced along the tip while he suckled. She arched her back, groaning. She entwined her fingers into the soft fur and tugged. A moan escaped her throat, deep, full of the excitement pounding in her chest.

Using his knee, he guided her legs apart. A shock of air whispered between her thighs. He kept kissing her. First her breast. Then her stomach. Slowly, he made his way to her lower abs, still pecking her skin with his velvet mouth. Each kiss was a puff of warmth on her flesh.

Never was she so aware of her blood racing through her veins and the flutters in her belly. She tried to keep her breaths even, but the arousal she was undergoing continued to coil her tight, as if she was a snake in the grass ready to strike— probably because he was tasting the hair between her legs, suckling her mound, worshiping this spot with tender kisses.

She couldn't help tugging at her own hair the longer he sexually tortured her with his smooth puckers. The heat between her legs was enormous—a fire only he could extinguish.

The moans kept leaving her throat. Her hips kept gyrating. Her back arched on its own.

Then his lips vanished. He was moving along her. His belly rested on hers. His mouth melted on her lips, and his tongue searched out hers. She gladly feasted on his wet flesh and wrapped her legs around his slim hips. The tip of his erection was feathering the excitement coursing between her thighs. He never stopped kissing her. She ran her nails along his back, taking his skin under her nails, needing to soak up everything about him and call him her own.

When his hard length eased into her very slowly, she

gasped. There was pain. Massive pain she knew to expect, and she only had part of him in her.

"Easy, Fire Woman," he softly said. "You must relax."

The hurt was a taste of Hell, but her excitement was a great hunger to devour him. She slipped her tongue back between his lips and kept tasting him, anything to ignore the pain. His length and girth were stretching her. Her flesh was locked tight about him where his movement tickled her insides.

Yes, the discomfort remained, but having him claiming her as his wife was too exciting to allow the pain to control her. She gripped his hips tighter with her legs and dug her nails deeper into his back.

His hiss was in her ear, for he, too, must be tasting the same pain thanks to her scratching and gouging, but he didn't tell her to stop. It was as if he wanted to also endure pain with the pleasure they were seeking together, that he refused to let her walk this road of discomfort alone.

At first, his thrusts were gentle, a stretching of her snug flesh. She couldn't get over the feel of his erection gliding in and out of her. He was coaxing her to open to him. His long length and thick girth teased her, even enticed her to enjoy what he was offering.

The pain remained, though, and as much pleasure as she was also receiving, she had to bite down on his shoulder to stop the wounded scream from leaving her throat.

"More," he whispered. "If it makes you feel better, more."

She almost gnawed on him while her legs clutched him tightly. Soon, though, the pure exquisite excitement smothered the pain. He was gliding easily into her, his heavy moans filling the wigwam.

Something was building inside her, heat hotter than the wood and rocks burning in the two fires. Everything was too sensitive—her skin, her toes, her fingers, her lips. She was balled tight and ready to burst wide open.

Just as the explosion consumed her, his own smothered cries in her hair joined hers. He took her far from where they lay, where she swore she touched the most unadulterated pleasure she'd ever experienced.

Chapter Thirteen: Heart of Soul

Now Edie understood the true definition of making love. What they had done wasn't a twenty-first century hook-up but two people coming together to create pure magic.

She snuggled deeper against the pit of Thunder Bear's arm and toyed with one of the claws on his necklace. Normally, she'd wonder about the time. Not tonight. All she knew was the stars were bright, and that was all that mattered.

The fire continued to burn. He'd added more logs and stones before they'd retired to the bed of fur robes. His heart quietly beat beneath her ear.

"Wife, why are you still awake?" he murmured, sleepiness in his voice. "Do you seek more pleasure?" There was a chuckle to his question. "Best to let yourself rest, for you will still be sore and not ready for me. Do not tempt me with your womanly charms."

Edie giggled.

"Remember . . ." His fingers tangled around her hair. "You are *Anishinaabe-kwe*. You must release the last of the white man's world and think of yourself as Fire Woman from now on. Think only in our language."

Edie stiffened. She peeked her head up, staring at him. "How did you know?"

"It's in your eyes. It was the first language you learned. The first customs you learned. If you are truly to be my wife, you must be *Anishinaabe* not only on the outside through your work, but also on the inside where your heart resides."

Hadn't she known she'd kiss Edie goodbye after he'd

claimed her?

"You are correct, husband," Fire Woman admitted. "I still think in English, besides Ojibway. And yes, I still think *Edie*. But I am your wife now. Fire Woman. As *Gitche Manidoo* willed it. I want to make you proud, not disappointed."

"You will never disappoint me. As I will never do anything to disappoint you." He kissed the top of her head.

Fire Woman peeked her head back up. "So you say?" She caressed his nipple.

"Why do you have a cunning look in your eyes?" There was humor to his tone, and a smile.

"Maybe I can go with you? The morning comes soon. To-night has been the only true moment we have had together ever since the summer." She bit down on her lower lip.

"I would give in to your request because I miss you, too." He stroked her cheek. "My heart aches for you as much as yours does for me, but if we are to have our own lodge, you have much to accomplish this winter. You must learn many more tasks that only your mother can teach you, and your women relations."

Disappointment steeped in Fire Woman's chest. "I under-stand. I do. But I will miss you, and . . . I am scared."

"Scared?" He hiked a brow. "What is there to fear?"

"That I will not be able to manage the winter. I read in the English books how harsh winter can be. I fear something may happen to you while you are gone. I—"

He set his finger over her lips. "Wife, do not fear, because if you fear, you are doubting my ability to protect and care for you—what I pledge to you as your husband. I am entrusting your family to care for you without me, and they will not dis-appoint. For they have cared for you this long, and look at how you have flourished."

"Yes, you are right." She should not have doubted him. She set her head back in the pit of his arm.

"Also, never mind your English books. They are written by white men. Instead, think of the stories passed down to you by our ancestors. Think of what you are learning here, too."

"You are correct." A smile tugged at her lips. "Mother and Father have never stayed at the back of the lodge before." She resumed drawing circles on his nipple.

His muscles tightened beneath her.

"What is it you are not telling me?" She poked his chest and giggled.

"I will admit I asked your parents to allow us some privacy tonight," he whispered.

Fire Woman froze. He had planned all of this. He came here with the intention of marrying her. "Is this what you spoke about to with Father this morning?"

"Yes."

Her frozen spine relaxed. She resumed tracing circles. "Part of me thought so, but I was not sure."

"I told him you are new to our ways. Understand, though, that we will be residing with your parents for a year. It is our way of life. You must accept this."

Well, every one of her female relations had to experience sharing their bed robes with their parents only lying across the way of the fire pit, so she could as well, although the mere thought was enough to heat her cheeks. A few times she'd heard Star Dancer and Swift Deer's soft moans and sighs. Even worse, her own parents. Light groans had also come from Kicking Elk and She Smiles.

Thunder Bear was right, though. Everyone did their best to offer the others privacy. And what they did was as natural as the flowing of the Rainy River and the waves on Lake of the Woods. The animals, fish, birds, and insects found no shame in what the Great Mother had created to ensure life continued.

"Yes, I understand."

"I know this is difficult for you, but this is how we live."

He shifted on the robes. "There will be many more tests you will face."

More tests. She clutched him tight. If she was to be as brave and strong as the other women, she would have to pass each one.

Even during the Freezing Over Moon, Swift Deer disappeared to scout. Fire Woman knew attacks mostly happened in the summer, but out in the wild, one could not be too cautious.

Star Dancer readied the morning meal.

Fire Woman had netted the fish earlier, her first chore of the day while she had cleaned up at the lake in the freezing water. She had only managed to wash the essentials because she could not immerse herself. Even ducking her hands had sent the most horrible burning pain of needles being shoved into her fingers.

Soon, she would have to break through the ice to gather water. Once *Biboon* arrived, she'd have to melt snow. For now, she was content to sit in the bosom of *Dagwaagin*, what her people referred to as fall.

Since the weather was too chilly to enjoy the outdoors, she took her food inside the wigwam where Thunder Bear sat. Heart heavy, she sank down beside him on the other rush mat. He'd leave once he'd eaten.

She jumped at the birdcall and whipped her gaze on Thunder Bear, who set aside his meal. That was a warning. Swift Deer was approaching with something or someone. Rustling from outside carried into the wigwam. Star Dancer was probably already halfway into the bush to greet her husband and find out what was amiss.

This was a vulnerable time when they separated into camps. Maybe Swift Deer was wounded.

Thunder Bear rose and grabbed his flintlock musket. "Stay

where you are, wife." He left the wigwam.

The birdcall came again, but not in warning.

Walks with a Limp rose and left. So did Woman of the Sky. Fire Woman remained put. Her husband had told her to stay, therefore she would not leave until he said otherwise. Laughter came from others. Sneers. They spoke rapidly.

Setting aside her meal she still held, Fire Woman inched to Thunder Bear's rush mat. Her family was taunting someone. They wouldn't taunt a Frenchman. Or another from a different clan.

Ice seemed to clutch her spine. The Dakota.

Here? Now? And only . . . one?

There'd been no alarm during Swift Deer's scout, which meant one individual Dakota was outside the wigwam, at the mercy of her family.

Although she'd vowed to become a true *Anishinaabe-kwe* of the eighteenth century, the fear pouring from her pounding heart said otherwise. She was of the twenty-first century—where killing another was considered murder, enemy or not.

Thank goodness she hadn't eaten anything, or she would have hurled. The talking continued.

"Ask him where the other *Little Snakes* are." This came from Mother.

"He is wounded. There is no loyalty among the *Little Snakes*. They must have left him for dead." The words belonged to Star Dancer.

"Enough." Kicking Elk had spoken. "Back to your chores. The men will speak about this."

A hint of annoyance prickled the back of Fire Woman's neck. The prickle grew scratchier when the rustling of leaves indicated the women had listened and were allowing the men to deal with the Dakota brave.

The wigwam flap fluttered. Mother entered. She took her spot at the warming fire and picked up her bowl of food.

Without saying a word, she ate. Her focus on Fire Woman's bowl said she should eat, too.

Fire Woman held back the questions her tongue demanded she ask, but she also shoveled the fish between her lips. Her stomach gurgled in protest, so she drank some water from her tin cup.

She was of the family and had to obey, as the women had. To survive, they operated as a unit, each with important tasks to administer or they could perish. As a scout, Swift Deer had simply been doing his job. Of course he hadn't let the Dakota brave go.

In spite of accepting the decision of the men, which would mean the loss of life for the Dakota brave, she found that swallowing the food was easier than swallowing her family's one and only solution to the invading presence.

"They will kill him tonight." Nonchalance and acceptance filled Mother's announcement.

"They . . . they're already done meeting?" Fire Woman almost dropped the wood she had gathered.

The Dakota brave was lashed to one of the many poplar trees. Shed of his clothing, he was as naked as the day he'd been born. Cuts covered his exposed skin, for each time someone passed him, they took a knife to his flesh. But the man had never winced. His chin remained out in defiance.

He wasn't painted, which meant he hadn't intended on making war. The clothes Fire Woman had witnessed stripped from him had been his buckskin shirt, leggings, and breech-clout. His moccasins had been tossed in the fire to burn. As for his fur robe, the gift had been given to Great-Grand-mother, Puckers Her Lips.

Earlier, the women had erected a quick dome-shaped lodge for the men to meet inside, since the only other small lodge available was where the women went to sit during their moon time, a place no man dared to enter, lest he desired to lose his medicine from the powers their womb blood left inside the interior.

"How do you know this?" Fire Woman gazed at her mother.

"It is what they always do." Mother simply shrugged. "They will keep torturing him until he speaks."

"How will they communicate if they don't understand the Dakota language?"

"They will sign. He will speak, for he knows it is not his life he is bargaining for, but a quick death, not a slow and torturous one."

The open wounds on the man punctured Fire Woman's heart. Blood seeped from each slit. His injuries hadn't been attended to, either. He stood using his one good leg. His ankle was the size of a balloon, meaning he had either sprained or broken it.

"How does he know he's bargaining for a quick death?"

"Because his people have done the same to ours." Mother's black brows furrowed. "Do you believe if the *Little Snakes* he traveled with had found us, they would have shown sympathy?" The gnashing of her lips said she was close to spitting. "They would have killed us all, even the children."

Fire Woman shuddered. She'd studied the wars between the Dakota and Ojibway. Yes, women and children were not spared, and even also brutally killed. She bowed her head.

"Do not have sympathy, daughter. He has none for you, even while he suffers." Mother's gaze glided to where the man stood.

Fire Woman again stole a peek at the Dakota brave. The fierceness in his slit-black eyes firing on Mother said if he could get a hold of his weapons he'd been relieved of, he'd launch his tomahawk into her head and take her scalp.

Mother spit in the direction of the Dakota.

Fire Woman glanced away.

They worked side by side until late afternoon before Mother stood and went inside the wigwam. With nobody around, Fire Woman stole another peek at the brave.

The man gazed back. The fiery hate he'd directed at Mother earlier wasn't present. His onyx eyes resembled warm black stones. He licked his lips, no doubt thirsty. Fire Woman peeked at the tin of water beside her. If she dared to offer him a sip, for sure the wrath of anger from her relations would drop on her head.

The man moved about in his stronghold of rawhide, as if fighting to find a comfortable position. His gaze landed on her cup. For the second time, he licked his lips.

I can't, she mouthed, although he probably didn't understand her.

Pleading filled his black eyes that were capable of producing murder. His pain was squeezing its way into her heart, begging for help, perhaps worried for his wife and children, and all the people back at his camp fretting about where he'd disappeared to.

Fire Woman bowed her head. She could end his suffering, even save him from torture, even being killed.

The last of the light hovered just below the tree line. Thunder Bear and Swift Deer had never departed as they were supposed to. The men had finally left the makeshift lodge to eat a late meal.

Fire Woman dished up food for Thunder Bear's bowls as was expected now that she was his wife. She entered the wigwam where he sat at the rush mat.

"*Meegwetch,* wife." He took the bowls from her.

She went back outside to get her own meal and joined him inside the wigwam. Mother and Father were already eating.

"What will happen to the Sioux?" she asked.

Father's one lifted brow was a warning not to ask further questions.

The stiffening of Thunder Bear's jawline more than indicated he disapproved of the inquiry. Then his jawline relaxed. Thoughtfulness rested in his black eyes. "Wife, do not make his fate any of your business. You have your own duties to attend to." His words were soft, a coaxing gentle reminder she was now a part of their world, not the twenty-first century she came from.

Fire Woman nodded. She would not say anything further, for to do so would shame her husband, their marriage, and herself in front of her family.

"Lay out my paints." Father gazed at Mother. "I will need them for tonight. Our son will need to borrow mine, as well, for his are back at his camp."

The gasp in Fire Woman's throat tried to claw its way to freedom. Painting themselves meant torture. For sure death would come for the Dakota brave tonight, as Mother had assumed. The man's fate was in Fire Woman's hands. She could not stand to the side and allow murder to happen.

She squeezed her eyes shut. Her heart screamed *no*. In her timeframe, they were not at war. Many of her Ojibway friends and family even visited the Dakota casinos in Minnesota. They joined in on the sun dances held. They attended the same powwows. They needed one another to fight the suppression the Indigenous People of North America experienced at the hand of the governments.

She could not let her relations kill an innocent man who'd done nothing. If she did, her conscience would strike her down for the rest of her living days, knowing she'd allowed a man to die and she'd done nothing to stop the murder.

CHAPTER FOURTEEN: SHE STANDS ALONE

Fire Woman's conscience refused to shut up. All evening while the others laughed and told stories, she could not participate because the thoughts kept racing through her mind. Even *Edie* desperately tried to surface, telling Fire Woman she did not belong in this century, and as a woman of the modern world, she must at least try to stop what was about to happen.

She wrung her hands. Her husband had shown so much understanding and patience to her adjustment and accepting her new world.

Still, the *jaasakiid* at the Grand Medicine had confirmed where she truly belonged by foretelling her return. He'd stressed she was only here to learn and to share the knowledge she acquired with the People living in the twenty-first century.

Fire Woman curled her fingers into the hem of her skirt and tugged at the fringes. She wasn't returning. She was Thunder Bear's wife and the adoptive daughter of Woman of the Sky and Walks with a Limp. Even though she was wife, daughter, grand-daughter, great-granddaughter, and friend to the *Anishinaabeg* who'd taken her in, she would not and could not stand aside and allow a helpless man, who had done nothing wrong, to die.

Fire Woman gathered her blanket and the deerskin cloth she washed every morning for her personal use because she loathed using leaves.

Nobody said anything as she vacated the wigwam. They probably assumed, since she held the cloth, she was answering nature's call. The outside fire continued to crackle and burn because someone kept feeding it. The Dakota brave remained lashed to the poplar tree. His eyes were closed, and he'd sunk into his bindings. He must have heard her because his lids opened fast and wide and he straightened tall with a slight grimace.

No brave wanted to be seen at their weakest. Naturally, he was prepared to show courage at whoever had stepped outside. He must have the hearing of an owl, because she'd used the lightest of footsteps. Maybe his name was related to *gookooko'oo*, but she would never know.

She glanced away from him and snuck into the men's lodge where she'd seen them take some weapons. A shiny, sharp object was not hard to find. Just as fast as she had ducked inside, she came back holding the handle of the knife in the tight grip of her fingers.

Curiosity reflected in the Dakota's eyes. By the tilt of his lips, maybe he was about to curl his mouth into a smirk. Fire Woman was not sure.

As she approached him, she glanced at her own wigwam. She held her finger over her lips, which was moot, because the Dakota probably did not understand the gesture. Fear was not present in his gaze, simply the same curiosity whenever he looked her way. She motioned at his bindings then pointed at the knife.

He gave a simple tilt of his head, as if saying he understood what she was about to do.

The battle continued to rage in Fire Woman's head — the wife of Thunder Bear demanded she remain loyal to her husband and family, but the *Edie* of the future stressed she could not allow the innocent man to be tortured and killed.

She held up the knife, somehow having done this without knowing so. Again, she peeked at the wigwam.

The Dakota said something, but she could not understand his words. However, the relief spilling from him was over-whelming enough to almost soak Fire Woman in its emotion.

She slid the knife beneath the rawhide wound tight to the tree. It took a bit of wiggling, but she finally got the blade through. The edge of the knife, being so sharp, easily sliced through the bindings.

The Dakota quickly shed the rawhide. Before Fire Woman could step away or blink, he seized her wrist. The pressure was enormous, and her fingers were forced open. The handle fell into the brave's palm. With a cunning smile, he held the tip beneath her chin.

His audacity, after she'd come here to spare his life, was a slap across Fire Woman's face. Her own foolishness mocked her with a loud jeer. She should have heeded Mother's warning of never trusting any of the *Little Snakes*.

With no choice but to go with him, Fire Woman attempted to offer the man support for his swollen ankle. They started away from the poplar tree and in the direction he pointed.

In seconds, the thick brush swamped them. Thank goodness the foliage had disappeared for the season, but the branches and twigs scratched Fire Woman's face. At least her arms had protection. As for him, being stripped of his clothes, he must have felt every scratch on his body. He hobbled along beside her. The knife remained thrust under her chin.

"I can't walk like this. You keep pricking me," she hissed.

He said something, and from his tone, he did not approve.

What if he raped and killed her? They were not going to the lake, but deeper into the interior. Naturally he avoided the water, because that was the first place her husband and family would look.

The blanket kept slipping from her shoulders while she

tried to help him walk, so she let the wool garment drop to the ground. He grunted and pointed for her to pick it back up. She growled and slung the darned thing over the crook in her arm. Fear should rack her with horrible shivers, but fiery heat gnashed her skin. She wasn't sure if she was angrier at herself or at him.

A whirring sound whipped through the air. The heavy weight of the brave hit Fire Woman at full force. She scrambled to hang on to the man, but his dead weight overpowered every muscle she possessed. They toppled over. When they hit the ground, the twigs and a branch dug into her backside. The man's wide eyes stared at her. Blood streamed from his scalp. A scream blew clear from her chest and out of her throat.

A horrible something was embedded in the back of the man's head. Blood pooled everywhere. She shoved at the brave. He rolled over. Some type of metal was rooted into his skull.

"Wife!" Thunder Bear roared.

Fire Woman scrambled to sit up. The skeleton-thick brush was shoved aside like a monstrous *wiindigo* kicking aside trees. Thunder Bear emerged. Even in the dark, the fury in his eyes said he was bordering on shaking her until he knocked her head clear off.

"Get up. Now," he spat out.

"Wh-where? Wh-where is everyone?" Fire Woman glanced around.

"Back at the camp." He motioned at her to rise.

"You came . . . came alone?"

"I do not need a white man's army to find one snake in a place that is my home. Nor do I need your family to aid me in finding you. I will *always* find you." The possessiveness of his words locked tight around Fire Woman's wrists.

She wobbled to her feet while snatching the fallen blanket.

She could not look at the dead Dakota man lying in the pile of leaves.

"I did not go with him of my own free will." She drew back her shoulders and thrust her chin.

"No, you did not. However, you cut him loose of your own free will." Thunder Bear reached down and picked up the knife. He sheathed the sharp object. "Come. Let us go."

His strong fingers were handcuffs encircling her wrist. He tugged.

Fire Woman had no choice but to stumble and follow behind him. His pace was swift yet graceful. Even in his obvious anger, he did not trample the dead leaves and foliage.

This was too unfair. She was a woman of the twenty-first century. What had he expected? For her to simply stand aside and allow a man who'd done nothing to die?

"I can—"

They stopped, and she almost crashed into his backside.

Thunder Bear whipped on his heel and raised one finger at her nose. "Have I not shown you nothing but understanding since you are new to our ways and have lived long with the white man?"

Fire Woman hadn't expected his kind of attack. She shuddered but nodded.

"Have I not been nothing but patient?"

Yes, he had been. Again, she nodded.

"Has not your family been patient? Your mother and father did not have to sleep at the back of the lodge last night, but they did, out of respect for me when I requested they do so, but they also did for you, because they love you and want you to be comfortable.

"For you to take advantage of the patience and understanding I gave you, that your family gave you, your parents gave you, you will be punished."

Fire Woman recoiled. The anger she'd directed at the

Dakota resurfaced. She opened her mouth but was silenced by his finger pinned against her lips.

"Not one word, wife. Remember that I am your husband. Understood?" He cocked his brow. "Do not force me to punish you further than what you will receive when we reach the camp."

She gasped. Yes, she expected her family to be angry. For Thunder Bear to be angry. But punished?

When Thunder Bear led them through the thick bush, silhouettes stood in the backdrop of the burning fire. He'd never had to face this kind of test before — anger hot enough to make his palm itch to slap his wife clear across the face.

How dare she choose a Sioux over her own husband and family? He was within his rights to dissolve their union, but he would not. Fire Woman was his wife until he took his last breath on the Great Mother. Nevertheless, allowing her deceit to go without punishment was unheard of.

Trust had been broken. Now Fire Woman must accept her fate and prove to him and her family they could once again count on her loyalty.

He glanced to the makeshift lodge the women had erected for the meeting. "Go there. It is where you will stay until I say otherwise."

Her sharp intake of breath pierced his ear.

"You heard me, wife." He craned his neck. His stare burned deep into hers. "Go. Now."

Fire Woman wrapped the blanket tighter around her shoulders. She stalked off to the small lodge.

Thunder Bear faced her family. His family. "She will be punished starting tonight. She is not to be acknowledged. She will feed and care for herself. I will leave her food so she can eat. She will be shunned until I say otherwise."

The family members nodded. The betrayal they felt was carved into their eyes and faces. Each one returned to the wigwam with the exception of Walks with a Limp.

He set his hand on Thunder Bear's shoulder. "My son, I am sorry—"

"There is no need to apologize on her behalf. You did not betray us. She did." Thunder Bear could not help the bitterness on his tongue.

"Yes, she did." Walks with a Limps' pitch dropped. "Remember, she comes from the land of the whites. She—"

"I am aware she does. I have shown her nothing but patience and understanding because of where she once resided, however, she is more than aware of what is expected of her."

"What of the captive?"

"He is dead. Let him lie where he is so the wolves can dine on what's left of his body. Snakes do not deserve a burial ceremony." Thunder Bear stalked to the wigwam to turn in.

All night Fire Woman tossed and turned. When she woke, there was no fire to keep her warm. She huddled as best as she could under her one wool blanket. The rustling and voices from outside said the camp was already awake.

Keeping the blanket wrapped tight, she edged from the small wigwam. As she softly walked to the outside fire to warm her chilled skin and calm her clattering teeth, nobody glanced at her. Always, there were greetings of good morning and something to say.

Even the children did not acknowledge her.

Fire Woman was aware of what was happening, for Shoomis and Koko had told her about shunning. How long this would go on, she had no clue. But having her new parents looking right through her as they conversed with other members of the family produced a sickening crack in Fire Woman's heart.

She turned toward the bush. If she was on her own, and banished to the small lodge, her first priority was not feeling sorry for herself. She had to survive. Fear prickled the back of her neck. Spending the day making everything she'd require to run a household was a must, or she'd perish. Maybe she might have to hunt, even though she had no clue how. Still, Mother had taught her how to spear and net fish.

"One last word, wife." Thunder Bear's voice filled her ear.

She quickly whipped around. Hope rose in her chest. Had he forgiven her?

His eyes remained a storm brewing on the horizon—dark and gloomy. "You will not be welcomed by your family or me any longer. To us, you are not here. A ghost and nothing more. The only help you will have is the food I will hunt for you. Nothing more."

Fire Woman parted her lips. "You are not trapping? You are not—"

"How am I to trap when you are dead, as far as your family is concerned?" He hiked a brow. His lips that had claimed her throat and made her his wife curled into a sneer. "I will have to feed you. It is my duty. Your mother is also providing you the essentials you will need to eat and clothe yourself."

The hope that had dropped to Fire Woman's feet rose a smidgen. He was not divorcing her, although he had every right to after she'd betrayed him. Mother was also helping.

"You will require the essentials to survive. You can spend the winter making what you will need. For the time being, I will paddle to my camp and gather my belongings to stay the winter here." He pointed. "Go. Now."

He turned and stalked off.

Fire Woman had not even a minute to let the anger gnaw at her insides over what she felt was injustice. There had been water to retrieve. Wood to gather. A hole to create in the tiny wigwam for smoke to billow from, since she required a fire inside or she'd freeze for another night.

She'd prove where her loyalty lay by constructing what she'd need for the wigwam she'd share with her husband once their year was up. This winter she was supposed to have begun making everything for their new home, anyway. With the minimal birch bark containers she had, Mother had also left fresh birch gathered during the Strawberry Moon that Fire Woman could begin shaping into bowls and other cooking supplies she'd require.

The snow would soon come, and she'd also need snowshoes, something she did not know how to construct. This was something Mother was supposed to have taught her.

Loneliness pooled around Fire Woman's heart. The sun had set. The voices from the other wigwam carried to where she stood alone. Thunder Bear had left. He probably would not be back until tomorrow or the next day.

Her belly grumbled. He was supposed to bring her food, but his trip meant she might not eat until he returned.

From the darkness, two fish were tossed her way. The dead creatures landed at her feet. Thunder Bear must have asked her family to feed her while he was gone. She had no spices, no dried berries, no mushrooms, no maple sugar, or anything to add to her dinner to make it flavorful. Well, pitying herself was pointless.

Yes, she could steal a canoe and try to find the portal, but she would not. Since childhood, she'd ached to live with her ancestors and wed a man brave and honorable enough to give her love to and open her legs for. Only quitters slunk off to pout and lick their wounded pride if all did not go their way. She'd prove to them she was *Anishinaabe-kwe*, strong and capable of not only accepting her punishment, but persevering.

Gratefulness was the way to look on her new plight. They

could have served her a harsher sentence by banishing her for good, leaving her to die in the bush somewhere.

Plus, what she'd done was no better than what the White Government had done to the Ojibway when first sailing over to this land — shoving their beliefs down the throats of the People by telling them their views and customs were wrong. She'd gone and done the unthinkable — thrust her twenty-first century principles that had been schooled by the whites onto her ancestors, instead of respecting their dealings with what they viewed as a problem.

The Ojibway believed in vengeance, not revenge. Vengeance was justice in the eyes of the People, while revenge was retaliation of ones wounded pride.

She gathered the fish. Acknowledging a *thank you* was also unnecessary. As far as her family was concerned, they were feeding something dead out in the darkness.

All she could do was pray that Thunder Bear would soon forgive her and allow her back to the lodge — where she knew she truly belonged, something she was born for.

CHAPTER FIFTEEN: RIDER IN THE SNOW

If anyone spied the rabbit, the furry critter would become a meal and then skinned for its plush white fur. So far, nobody had spotted the beautiful animal. Every day the bunny came to Fire Woman for the dried berries she offered. At least Mother had shown more pity and had given Fire Woman what she had worked hard on during the fall. She even had wild rice to eat, something else she'd helped to harvest and prepare.

Her weight had dropped. Conserving food was imperative, although Thunder Bear left her something to cook whenever he hunted. The nights were long and cold. Sleeping together to keep warm was a must for families, and she had nobody to seek body warmth from.

The hunger wasn't the worst part of the winter. Christmas should be happening any day. Or maybe the special holiday had already passed. No matter, being without her real family and having to go it alone, nobody to speak to, was emptying her heart of any warmth left inside.

This afternoon, she'd kill for a present, a decorated tree, or even a simple mug of eggnog.

The promise she'd made to herself goaded her to keep persevering. By the time her punishment was up, how she'd handled herself would fill her family with pride, as opposed to taking the easy way out by fleeing in search of the portal.

She left the ration of berries outside of her wigwam and straightened. One morning, snowshoes had magically appeared outside the lodge. She'd take a walk deep in the woods for something to do before the sun set for the long evening and while her food cooked, anything to kill the loneliness since she hadn't talked to her husband or family after her banishment.

"Greetings! Greetings!" The voice belonged to Charlot.

Fire Woman set aside her snowshoes and peered into the bush. Stalking through the snow was Charlot. A big pack rested on his back.

"Charlot," she called out.

"What is this?" He came through the last of the bush, pointing at the small lodge. "Are you staying in there?"

Fire Woman wasn't about to embarrass herself by admitting she'd been banished. Let him think her moon time had arrived and she was coming from the women's lodge, even though women were to remain inside. "For now," she simply replied. "I did not expect you. Are you not trapping?"

His laugh was jovial. "It is Christmas. I am on my way to Fort St. Pierre for the festivities. I always stay there until the new year."

"How has your trapping gone?" She motioned at the wigwam to invite him in for a hot drink and some food.

"Very well, *ma chérie*. I have heard, though, that you are . . . well, facing some trouble." He offered a sheepish smile.

Why had she assumed only the Internet could provide quick information to the world? The moccasin telegraph was just as bad. No doubt Thunder Bear's family had spread the word of what she'd done. Come the Sugarbushing Moon, she'd face more ridiculing from the rest of the camp when they regrouped, or maybe even scorn.

Something tightened around her heart. Reality punched her cheek. Understanding was blinking on and off in front of her eyes — why Thunder Bear had served such a punishment. As his wife, he also faced embarrassment, scorn, and ridicule over what she'd done. She'd shamed him.

"Do not look so forlorn." Charlot set down his big pack. "I told you many times, you are a woman raised in the east among my people. Of course you can't sympathize with their war or their methods of dispatching of their enemy. This is their fight. Not mine. Not yours."

"I am his wife." Fire Woman raised her chin. "I was wrong—"

"You were not wrong. I thought about you. I know this festive season would bring you heartache since you are far from your family, so I brought you a Christmas present."

"For me?" Fire Woman set her hand on her chest that began to brighten.

"*Oui*. For you."

"Are you staying or continuing on your journey?" Excitement joined the blood rippling through her veins. "Please, come in and eat."

"Food sounds wonderful. I always stop in to see my *Saulter* friends before I enjoy a wonderful break until the New Year." He opened his pack. "I have already cashed in my pelts at Fort St. Charles."

"Why did you not stay there?"

"As I said, I always visit my *Saulter* friends first. Furthermore, I prefer the celebration at Fort St. Pierre." He withdrew a frying pan, a tin cup, and a tin plate.

Fire Woman almost dropped from relief. She'd taken to cooking her food using a four-way split log with kindling burning the interior slowly, what Mother had called a fire log. Inside the four-way split, she'd immerse her meat or fish to roast slowly, and slow boil her wild rice on top.

"While the food is cooking, I was going to take a walk." She motioned at the thick log standing upright where the deer meat simmered. "I only made enough for myself. You may eat first. You have traveled a long way. I will ready another piece for myself."

Snowshoes crunching on the snow carried to where they stood.

Fire Woman glanced to where her husband glided on top of the deep snow that easily reached thigh-level.

"She is a banished woman," he told Charlot. "Do not speak to her. You always honor our ways. I ask you to do so again."

Charlot nodded. He glanced at Fire Woman. "I never interfere with their customs, as do my allies. I am sorry."

She lowered her head. "Do not apologize. I did wrong—"

"You did nothing wrong, *ma chérie*. Remember this—divorce is allowed in their world. I can always take you with me back to your family." Charlot hefted his pack, motioned at the presents he'd left, and stalked toward Thunder Bear. "I come to join you for the night before I set off to the fort in the morning for the festivities."

"Yes, the celebration of the birth of your *manidoo*," Thunder Bear replied. "Join them. They will be happy to see you."

While Charlot kept walking toward the wigwam, Thunder Bear continued his trek across the snow to where Fire Woman stood.

He stopped and folded his arms. The bearskin robe swathing his body was a sight to behold. She'd seen him many times in the regal fur blanket. The massive head served as his hood. "You are not supposed to speak to anyone. This is part of your punishment."

"Charlot is not *Anishinaabe*. I did not think it was wrong." She held his stare. Her heart pumped too quickly. Blood rushed to her head, toes, and fingers.

"He is a man we have befriended. He visits us often. Therefore, you cannot speak to him." The black of his irises darkened to a moonless night of pure ice. Something else flickered there that matched the flames of the fire burning in her lodge.

Her desire was great for him.

His desire for her was also great, given the boldness of his gaze stroking her body from her mukluks to the top of her head.

"I understand, husband." She had vowed to show her relations she could withstand the punishment of banishment, instead of sulking off in self-pity.

"You never once attempted to find the dancing flames," he murmured.

"I am your wife." She drew back her shoulders. "It takes a woman of courage, strength, and humility to possess such a man. I disappointed you once. I will not do so again."

Plus, she had a good hunch he would've been hot on her trail if she had dared to tuck her tail between her legs and run to the portal like a pouting child, sulking because she had been spanked, and rightly so for daring to allow her beliefs to interfere with those of the community.

In this new world, community was everything, not individual desires and wants. Her people had flourished for time immemorial operating in this manner. It had been the white man's government who'd destroyed the structure, beliefs, and customs of the Ojibway nation that had spawned the almost-devastation of her people in the present time.

The narrowness of Thunder Bear's eyes softened. He reached out. His finger touched her cheek like a soft feather.

Fire Woman shivered.

"Your white man celebration is soon to happen. I knew you would be sad, for we do not share in their revelry and worship of this *manidoo*. Feed me, wife."

He turned and entered the wigwam.

Fire Woman's heart almost popped from her chest. She quickly dashed about, making the final preparations for his meal.

Once she had his food cooked and her own slice of deer meat roasting in the log, she carried the meal inside on the new tin plate. She'd also packed snow in the tin mug to boil water for his spruce tea.

The lodge was small, and the heat plentiful. She set the plate and cup beside him. He had removed his robe to reveal his buckskin shirt, leggings, and mukluks. The deerskin mittens were also off to the side.

"Join me. There is enough to satisfy us while the rest of the meal cooks." He motioned at the burning fire. The smoke billowed to the opening at the top.

"*Meegwetch.*" She removed her blanket and sat adjacent from him on the rush mat. "I must also thank you again for bringing me food faithfully."

He bit into the piece of deer meat, nodding.

From his chewing, she knew he was relishing the morsel of food.

"It is my duty, something I will always do. I will never let you go hungry. I will starve first to feed you and our children we will eventually have."

The word *children* created insurmountable warmth on Fire Woman's face and between her legs. She set her hand on her stomach. Since she had already finished her moon time, a child had yet to grow inside her. But if Thunder Bear stayed the night . . .

He held up the plate.

Fire Woman took a piece of the deer meat.

"Yes, I saw you enter the women's lodge." His face and features appeared bright, as if he was not disappointed. "We will have one. This I know."

Was he hinting of staying the night? She licked her lips.

"Eat, wife. You will need your energy." His slim lips formed a smile more delicious and juicier than the succulent meat Fire Woman chewed.

Thunder Bear finished his second cup of spruce tea while his wife cleaned up after their meal. Staying away from her had been pure torture, especially after only having one night alone as a true couple. His patience had paid off. Not once had Fire Woman attempted to flee to the dancing flames from where she had first appeared. Nor had she tried to speak to anyone. With true courage, she had acknowledged her punishment, and had even reflected on her transgression.

If not for the custom of living with his wife's parents for the first year, he would welcome the small lodge they occupied. Come the morning, much to his disappointment, they'd have to move her belongings back to the main lodge.

They had one night to enjoy themselves without any embarrassment or apprehension on his wife's part.

Fire Woman reentered the wigwam. She stored away the possessions used to make their meal. While doing so, she presented her behind to him. He could not help running his tongue along his lower lip at the offer she presented.

"You know I must resume my intended duty before you were punished." He unbound his braids.

Fire Woman turned. Her delicate features sank, but as quickly, she sharpened her sagging jaw and nodded. "I understand. Charlot informed me he will return to trapping after the festivities are finished at the fort."

"You will be well cared for while I am gone," he reassured her as delicately as possible. "I have hunted enough meat to keep you and your parents fed. Although your father's leg is lame, he will hunt to replenish the food. Your mother remains healthy even after his injury."

"I do not doubt of my father's ability." Fire Woman sank down beside him on the rush mat.

"The worst is yet to come." He did not want to frighten her, but she had to know the reality of *Biboon*'s harsh reign. "If you think the snow is deep now, it is not. The weather will grow harsher and colder. The snowfall will seem endless. You will feel some hunger, your belly not fully satisfied, but you will not starve. You were wise to ration the food I brought you."

"I learned of this from the white man's books in school. I read much on this century."

He rubbed his teeth together. Where was this strange place she spoke about? She was not from the east of that, he was sure. She was forward, somewhere ahead of him on the red road in his vision. The dancing flames had allowed her to move backward, as the Thunderbirds had promised. He could not ask, either, for during his vision quest, the mighty beings had warned him not to. Yet he had a good hunch she knew many things about the present in which he lived in.

Keeping her safe was imperative, something the Thunderbirds had demanded of him, no matter the cost, even his own life. The mighty beings had something in store for her, some reason they had instructed him to ensure her safety.

He did what his wife liked to do and entwined their fingers. This brought a smile prettier than the buttercups he'd first presented to her when she'd walked through the flames. He leaned in and slid his mouth over hers. The lushness of her lips was an ache beating in his heart. Their time apart had been his guts being ripped from his stomach.

To touch her again, kiss her again, and smell her again was producing luxurious sensations across his skin. Her mouth eagerly tasting his said she'd also suffered for him during her exile. His fingers cried out for him to undress her.

He slid his hand up her skirt, caressing her leg along the way until he reached her hip. Her lush flesh was smoother than doe skin beneath his palm. He walked his fingers past her hip and to her firm buttock that flexed under his fingertips. Her tongue became a furious exploration of his mouth.

Such hunger. Such want.

His own excitement intensified. His hard flesh ached to be within her, pumping deep and fast. But the ache would have to wait, because he wanted to introduce his wife to other pleasures that could be enjoyed on their bed of robes.

CHAPTER SIXTEEN: WILD FLOWER

Fire Woman tilted her head back and let her husband feast on her throat with suckles and licks. His tongue was hotter than a flame, wet and delicious, coaxing luxurious excitement to surface between her legs. The familiar throb she'd experienced when they'd first come together teased her clit.

She couldn't help her English thoughts, because during times like this, it was easier to think in modern terms than the sweet, melodic language of her ancestors. Her friends had bragged about the wonders they'd encountered when a guy went down on them. She couldn't wait to know first-hand what they'd raved about.

Thunder Bear's hand was no longer on her hip but trailing to the thatch of hair she'd only allowed him to touch. She guided her thighs apart. His lips left her throat and formed a path of kisses to her breasts. She grasped his long strands of hair and explored his satin-like locks.

He groaned. His teeth captured her nipple, and he lightly nibbled. The taunting suckles produced shivers of exhilaration down Fire Woman's back. Part of her ached for him to hurry and reach the place she yearned for him to taste with his mouth, but she held her breath and let him take his sweet time, for each kiss and nibble was complete and utter heaven.

His fingers skated along her belly. He stroked her skin with feather-like caresses, the teasing kind that tickled and generated goosebumps. The squeal left her mouth. She lay on her back while he continued to rain licks and kisses on her breasts.

Her dress was gathered almost to her neck. He unfastened

the sleeves and slipped them from her arms. She wriggled out of the garment, and he shucked it aside. The fire reached her naked flesh, surrounding her in heat that her skin was also producing.

Thunder Bear doffed his shirt and tossed it on her dress. Then he stood and worked on his leggings. She moved onto her elbows. Her gaze ate up his sexy form of lean muscles and bronzed skin. He unfastened his breechclout. She lowered her gaze to his hard cock and tight balls. He shifted to his knees and settled between her legs.

Anticipation pounded in her chest. She wet her lips, shivering.

He kissed the flesh just above her pussy hairs. The softness of his lips and light breaths dusting her skin was an erotic awakening she'd never felt before. Her clit throbbed, aching for his touch. With his tongue, he traced a wet trail to her pussy, leaving delicious licks on her flesh. When he came upon her womanly lips, she held her breath. The air leaving his mouth was hot and moist, heating her skin. He pressed his mouth on her pussy and kissed the hairs.

Every muscle constricted, and her aching clit became a yearning throb. The more he teased her pussy with his breaths, the more she couldn't help constricting her thighs. Being on her back, she wanted to rise and see what he was doing. She did move onto her elbows. The admiration in his eyes as he gazed at her nest of hairs drew a deep moan from her.

He glanced her way. His tongue came out and parted her lips. She sucked in a breath. The tip of his wet flesh hit her clit. A million jolts of electricity shot through her limbs. The pleasure was like being draped in sheets of satin. She dropped her head back on the robes and gazed up at the round ceiling of the wigwam.

His licks were slow, circling around her hard flesh, never

quite touching, only teasing. She dug her nails into his long strands of hair and yanked. What he lavished on her was a true awakening of eroticism. She couldn't get over the excitement raging through her. He was lapping at every region except the one spot where she ached for him to touch.

Now she knew what it meant to be left begging and pleading. She had to bite down on her lower lip to stop herself from screaming at him to please lick her clit.

Finally, the tip of his tongue lapped at the spot she'd been yearning for him to taste. She came close to overheating. Every nerve screamed with delight. She wrapped her legs around his strong shoulders and held him tight. The pleasure he rained on her was enough to overwhelm her. She thrashed beneath the delicious tormenting his tongue inflicted on her. The feelings were overpowering, consuming her from the inside, her skin reacting with goosepimples. Shivers rode her spine.

The ecstatic pleasure captured her in its wet heat, and the most wonderful sensations consumed her.

Thunder Bear trailed his fingers along Fire Woman's bare skin. She lay in the pit of his arm. Her breaths dusted his chest with warmth. His ache for her was great, but she needed time to revel in what she'd experienced. He also needed time to reflect.

Tasting her womanly essence had been true gratification. Always, he wanted to see that smile on her face — the pleasure of potent ecstasy when she'd succumbed to his tongue. Her palm was on his stomach, moving in slow circles.

He pecked the top of her head. The fire crackled and popped. The peaceful aroma of burning wood drifted under his nose. A silhouette of dancing flames lined the one birch wall.

How he loathed to leave her, but he had to trap the precious furs to gain more ammunition. He also wanted to trade for more of the white man's materials to ease his wife's burden around their lodge, such as knives for skinning and pots to make cooking easier. There were some women who also made skirts and tops from the bolts of fabric supplied at the forts. Fire Woman deserved some pretty beads to decorate her outfits and his.

Some of the men had taken a shine to the fire water. Not him. The strange brew was pure poison, causing his people to act outrageously while under the spell of whatever was in the liquid.

"The fire water is a bad drink," he murmured.

Fire Woman stiffened.

He'd sensed by bringing up the topic he'd get this reaction. She knew things about what would happen to them now that the white man had invaded Turtle Island. If only he could ask her what lay ahead for the People—but he could not go against the wishes of the Thunderbirds.

"I want you again." He brushed his lips against her silky hair.

"Me, too." Her whisper was on his nipple. She shifted. Her dark eyes peeked at him.

He used his finger to trace her nose with its lovely smooth tip. She moved up on her elbow. Her lips claimed his. To have her initiating their joining raised goosebumps on Thunder Bear's skin and even plumped his ego. He wrapped his arms around her sleek waist and pulled her against him. Her nipples were alive, the hard peaks pressing on his chest. He glided his fingers along her smooth back. His palm filled with electrical excitement from the softness of her skin. He reached her firm buttock and moved his hand in a circular motion.

She groaned into his mouth while still tasting his tongue with her own. He'd had a full look at her ripe pink flesh earlier. Now he yearned to see the delicious hole between her buttocks. He couldn't resist toying with her cleft. Her cheeks tightened, and her kiss shifted from sensual licks to fervent strokes. He drew his finger down her crack. She squirmed. Another groan from her filled his mouth.

He slipped his hand from between her cheeks and rolled them over. She lay flat on her back, gazing up at him. Her tongue came out, and she wet her lips. How he yearned to fill her mouth with his hard flesh, but his erection demanded he be inside her.

"Move on to your hands and knees," he whispered.

Her dark eyes sparkled. She obeyed faster than he had anticipated. Her eagerness was stroking his hardness. When she presented her ass to him, the heart shape of her behind toyed with his already throbbing tip. He situated himself over her in a squatting position. The pink of her asshole dared him to penetrate her, but that would be for another time. He simply wanted to watch her delicate hole pucker and flex while he pumped inside her tight wetness.

She peeked at him over her shoulder. Her long hair feathered the bed of robes. The flames from the fire played along the contours of her beautiful face. He could not thank *Gitche Manidoo* enough for bringing this stunning woman into his life, who was now his wife. He would please her in every way possible and cherish each moment of the life they would spend together. Most of all, he ached to watch her grow with their child in her belly.

The masculine hunger tearing through him demanded he ride her and truly claim her. He entered her tight depths and groaned. She had engulfed his erection with her wet heat, claiming him instead. She also never looked away but kept peeking at him. Her eyes were fiercer than the burning flames that scorched the logs in the pit. Truly, she was fire, capable of heating him to a melting point, or burning him with deep scars and horrific wounds like when she had betrayed him by cutting the Sioux loose.

Never would she know the power she possessed over him.

His hardness ached beyond belief, and although he wished to move slowly, he could not help his deep pumps and quick thrusts. The need to taste every inch of her was consuming him.

She no longer gazed his way. Her head was bowed, and her sweet moans filled the small lodge as she moved along his length. He held her by the hips, gliding back and forth. She continued to grip him with her wet flesh, raising her ass higher. Her hole was puckering, and he could not help fingering the delicate spot.

A scream came from her.

His own moans joined her, for she had devoured him with her heat once again.

Fire Woman.

The Thunderbirds had chosen her name well.

The blue jays that had not migrated south squawked outside the lodge. Thunder Bear's lids flickered. Morning was upon them. The animals were telling them to wake and rise for the day.

Fire Woman remained cuddled in his embrace. To leave her to trap was an ache in his heart. He would enjoy his morning meal and each moment with her until he had to depart. He pecked her cheek. She murmured something. Then her lashes fluttered. The big smile she presented said she was happy to wake in his arms.

"It is time to rise." He again pecked her cheek.

"Hmm . . . are you hungry?" A twinkle sparkled in her eyes. She wrapped her legs around his.

"Very hungry. I do not wish to get up, but it is time."

"Yes, it is. I will make you a big meal before you start your journey."

"A big meal sounds excellent."

While she donned her clothing and went out to relieve herself, he wrapped his bear robe around himself to poke the coals in what was left of the fire. Once he added some wood, the flames began heating the interior. By then she had returned. He left her to ready everything for cooking, which would be the leftovers from last night and more wild rice.

The day was crisp, a dry cold that he preferred. Already, the cooking log was lit. By the time he hunted some small game for her to dine on tonight and some fresh game for himself, his food would be ready. The sun hadn't quite risen yet. Dawn was upon them.

He dressed and retrieved his bow and arrow. Once he had fastened his snowshoes, he was off into the bush, walking until he came to the spot he sought — the tracks of a grouse on the edge of the spruce stand. They burrowed beneath the snow to stay warm, but at this time of day, the bird would be seeking food. The grounded creature's tracks trailed through the underbrush. His gaze traveled to one feather on the snow and another on a twig, most likely at the edge of its trail.

He withdrew an arrow from his quiver. His gun remained back at the lodge, because he would not waste his precious ammunition on a bird that he could just as easily kill with his bow and arrow. He sighted the arrow and stepped forward, ensuring he set his snowshoes down hard while waiting for the flush, the best time to catch them by stepping toward the sound.

His stamping startled one hiding in the skeletal underbrush. The bird ran as it always did before taking flight. He released the arrow. It whirled through the air and captured the bird, which fell to the ground. He had one more to catch for himself. This grouse was for his wife to enjoy for her evening meal after he was long gone.

He squatted over the fallen bird and stroked its feathers. The song came softly from his throat, a beautiful prayer his father had taught him to sing for each lovely creature that had given its life so he could feed his family.

The air was a refreshing coolness on his skin, nature's way of naturally renewing his body with energy. He stroked the bird's feathers one more time before setting it in his *gash-kibidaagan*.

Later, when he returned to the lodge with his game, the smoldering flames in the upright log were burning down. This meant his meal was ready. He entered the small wigwam.

A rabbit was snacking on dried berries. The furry creature's ears straightened. It darted between his legs and dashed outside.

"Wife?" He glanced behind him.

"I . . ." Fire Woman smoothed her dress. She had removed her blanket and sat before the burning fire. "He kept me company during my banishment, so I feed him."

Thunder Bear could not help his frown. "You know our ways. He must provide for himself as the circle dictates."

"I know." Red stained her cheeks. She bowed her head. "Food is precious, especially during the winter."

"I am glad you found company during your lonely time from us, but you cannot keep feeding him. He is responsible for feeding himself, as I have a responsibility to feed you."

"It is only one rabbit." Pleading reflected in her eyes. "Where I come from, we keep them as pets."

"Pets? Only dogs are kept as such, for they are useful in our hunts and travels." He removed the two grouse from his bandolier bag. "These are for you. I will take one with me for my evening meal tonight."

"I will have it cleaned and prepared for you before you leave." She held out the tin plate. "For you. Some food, my handsome husband." The red had vanished from her cheeks. Admiration shone in her gaze.

He removed his fur, set aside his quiver and bow, hung his *gashkibidaagan,* and took a seat beside her. "Thank you." He accepted the tin of food. "You may keep the rabbit, but understand, your parents may say otherwise."

"You are so good to me." She leaned in and pecked his cheek. "I knew you would understand."

"Understand?" He arched his brow and bit into the delicious leftover fish. "I know the rabbit will make you happy. If you are happy, then I am happy."

He knew how much she enjoyed the white man's materials, so he was smart in trading for many of such luxuries at the fort.

Chapter Seventeen: Born into This

The blizzard came out of nowhere and did not cease. Fire Woman had lost track of how long the endless snowfall had lasted so far. They were trapped inside the wigwam, only leaving for the bare necessities, such as relieving themselves. Without snowshoes, the white stuff was a good waist high.

Walks with a Limp was supposed to replenish their meat, which he'd been unable to do. He'd tried twice, but the snowstorm proved merciless. They were reduced to eating the pemmican, dried berries, and wild rice.

Thank goodness the men had seen to stockpiling firewood before winter had set in.

Fire Woman shivered. She had read about families boiling their moccasins and softening bark in the heated water to eat, just as Charlot and his father had been forced to do. Hopefully, life for them would not come to that. But if not this winter, starvation could come the following year, or the next.

There was no game to hunt anyway. The animals were hard to find because they were doing the same thing—seeking shelter from the blizzard. At least the rabbit she'd named White One kept the children amused. They loved playing with the fluffy creature who had found a home in the lodge. *May we not be reduced to eating the precious pet.* Nor could she stop her family if that was what they decided on.

This was the true life of her people. She'd interfered once with her modern-day beliefs, but she would not do so again. Sure, it was easy to become an animal activist in the twenty-first century by simply purchasing food at a grocery store.

Not out here, deep in the wilderness, where surviving meant hunting animals to eat and skinning them for their fur to keep warm. If they did not, they'd die. It was as simple as that.

She glanced at the children, who were holding their pet. They had seen dogs brought down and eaten for special ceremonies. This meant they'd understand if White One had to be honored as their next meal.

He Paddles on the Crooked River had told many stories while they'd huddled around the fire. He'd called this the time *when the spirits sleep*. To tell stories while *manidoog* were awake was to invite malevolence into their lodge. If her adoptive great-grandparents and grandparents respected the instructions passed down by their ancestors, *Gitche Manidoo* and *Biboon* might pity them.

Her gaze wandered to the lodge opening. Thunder Bear was out there somewhere. She put her hands together in prayer. *May the spirits care for him, Swift Deer, and Charlot.*

The blizzard continued to rage on. Fishing through the ice was moot because too much snow covered the lake, making digging to create a hole impossible. Fire Woman's stomach growled. She ate the last of her bowl of wild rice. One meal a day, and not enough to sustain her.

The children had stopped playing with White One and cried for more food.

Walks with a Limp stood. "If I do not seek an animal, we will starve. I must try." He pointed at what was left of their rations. Everyone was leaner in the winter, and he'd lost more weight than usual. "I must go while I still have the strength. We cannot take the chance. The *wiindigoog* could show here any day. This is when they arrive, during the harshest times."

Fire Woman shivered. She did not want to witness cannibalism. "I will accompany you. I am not a mother who must care for children. I am not a grandmother who must teach the children. I am not with child. I am young and strong. I can help you."

Walks with a Limp looked to the grandfathers.

"I will go," Kicking Elk, Woman of the Sky's father, announced. He gazed at Fire Woman. "Your offer is honorable and generous, but because you are young and strong, and newly married, we need your eventual child to ensure the circle continues. Sit. Please."

Fire Woman wrapped her arms around the crying Little Acorn. She nodded, although words of protest sat on the edge of her tongue. Kicking Elk was no longer in his prime, a grandfather to Little Acorn and Frog Jumper.

"We will smoke and pray. The smoke will carry our prayers to *Gitche Manidoo* who will hear our cries." Kicking Elk went to one of his bags hanging on the lodge pole and withdrew his pipe.

Nobody spoke about the length of time Walks with a Limp and Kicking Elk had been gone. Fire Woman was not sure whether to say their names and voice her worries was taboo. *Biboon* did show some mercy. One day there wasn't snow, but the following day the snow came again at full force.

The last of their rations had dwindled to emptiness. Constant cries came from the children. Fire Woman kept her arms around Frog Jumper. Little Acorn was cuddled against her mother.

Outside, the wind continued to howl, a presence she had grown accustomed to ever since the storm had appeared, refusing to leave.

"He must do what he must do," Great-Grandfather proclaimed. "*Biboon* knows he must take life, for new life comes once he rests and allows his brother to wake." He glanced to the rabbit.

Fire Woman's heart tightened.

A tear slid from the old man's right eye. "You, my friend, have proven much courage." He picked up White One. The rabbit's ears twitched. He petted the animal's fur. "It breaks my heart to ask you to feed us, for you have kept my grandchildren amused during this difficult time. But now I ask one more thing from you, my little friend. The song will calm you. It is the song that brings the four-legged creatures to us."

He kissed the top of the rabbit's head and hummed. His singing grew louder. White One stared, as if in a trance. Not even his long ears twitched.

He Paddles on the Crooked River held out his hand.

Puckers Her Lips reached into a bag and withdrew a slim deer hide rope. She shuffled to her husband and handed it to him.

Fire Woman hugged Frog Jumper tighter. Fear and dread beat hard in her chest.

Great-Grandfather kept singing. His soft words were a lullaby. White One never protested but remained in the crook of the old man's arms, strange for a beautiful creature of prey whose natural instinct was not to be held, for being held meant death. Great-Grandfather wrapped the rope around White One's neck.

Fire Woman closed her eyes. A loud scream tore through the wigwam. She'd heard a rabbit scream once when she'd been cutting grass and had put the baby bunny back into safe shelter since he'd been hopping around, scared up by the sound of the lawn mower. Now the terrible cry had dug into her ears.

Great-Grandpa kept singing. His words were of bravery, of honor, of respect, and of love.

The only sound left was the crackling and popping coming from the fire.

Fire Woman's lids flickered.

White One lay limp in Great-Grandfather's arms. Tears

streamed down the old man's wrinkled face. He glanced up at her. "*Gitche Manidoo* brought your friend to you. Your friend already knew his fate, and he showed bravery by continuing to come to your lodge every single day.

"He has given his life so you can live. Honor him by eating his meat. Honor him by wearing his flesh on your hands. Honor him by lining his fur inside your mittens to keep your hands warm. Honor him by decorating your braids with his feet so all will know what he did for you.

"We do not kill to kill." He shook his head. "The porcupine quills you see decorating our shirts and dresses, the bear robe your husband drapes around himself, the clothing covering your body — all that you see in this lodge came from the four-legged beings. To honor them, we wear and use what they have selflessly shared. That is why everything must be used from an animal. Everything. They teach us bravery and humility by sacrificing themselves. In turn, we sing to them, thanking them for their selflessness, for they understand how the circle operates. They know their role while physically living on the Great Mother, just as we do."

He held out the animal to Woman of the Sky. "This will feed us until they return. With a deer. I have seen this."

Fire Woman closed her eyes. She'd witnessed the death of her pet — yet she was not angry or sad. The song Great-Grandfather had sung had aroused a spiritual connection between them and White One. She now fully understood why individualism was frowned upon. This was why community came first. This was why everyone did their jobs required of them, and did them well. She could fully accept their way of life now. Truly accept each custom and ritual.

Once Mother skinned the animal, Fire Woman would begin working on new mittens lined with fur to honor White One.

They'd gone two days without food after eating White One's meat. The call from outside the wigwam during a lull in the cries of the wind forced Fire Woman from her sleeping spot. The sun had sunk, and she'd been lulling Frog Jumper to sleep.

Woman of the Sky leapt to her feet. She reached for her snowshoes and wrapped a fur robe around herself. Fire Woman joined her mother. They stepped outside to brittle cold that dug its way into her bones. Through the darkness and softly falling snow, three silhouettes appeared.

Her heart sang a song of happiness. There were her father, grandfather, and . . . even Charlot accompanied them. They were carrying parts of a carcass on their backs. Now the women would take over.

"We would have been here sooner, but we had to bleed it and gut it first," Charlot called out.

"A full day traveling to get here," Walks with a Limp muttered. "Wife, take the animal so I may rest."

"Of course." Woman of the Sky removed the pack from her husband's back.

Fire Woman quickly removed the other wrapped pack on her grandfather's back. The older man was breathless. She kissed his cheek. "Come. Let me take your clothing and dry them. Then you can sit by the fire and warm yourself. Thank you, Grandfather. Thank you."

Kicking Elk smiled and trudged to the wigwam.

The animal was somewhat frozen. They would have to start a fire outside where they'd kept the area next to the lodge trampled and packed. Once the deer had thawed, which would not take as long since the men had cut the animal into nine pieces, the women could begin the skinning process.

Limbs weakened and her belly grumbling, Fire Woman set to work, no matter that it was dark outside. They had to eat.

She first gathered more wood to build the fire. Then they

set up the drying racks to hang the nine pieces from. They had to keep careful watch so the animal did not cook, but merely thawed. She refused to ruin the precious pelt and skin they would use, along with the brain and marrow, since the men had already removed the vital organs.

The deer stared at her. His antlers would be of good use to them. She bowed her head. "Thank you for allowing my father and grandfather to hunt you." This type of weather was known as the starving time. Tracking an animal was next to impossible, because the four-footed beings left in search of food for themselves.

Well into the next day she kept working beside her mother, Star Dancer, and She Smiles, while Puckers Her Lips watched the children.

The evening meal was cooked. When Fire Woman sat down to enjoy the delicious meat, never was she so thankful.

"You are tired. Rest," Charlot suggested in a hushed voice.

"I must eat first. I am so hungry." But Fire Woman would not gluttonize herself. There were others who also needed food. "Have you seen my husband? Or my uncle?"

Charlot shook his head. "Have no fear. Thunder Bear and Swift Deer will be fine. They have done this for many winters now."

"How did my grandfather and father come upon you?" She bit into another delicious morsel.

"They know where I trap. I, too, was snowbound. Your winter maker is showing no mercy. I was down to the last of my rations."

"You have a lodge?"

"*Oui.* When you trap, a lodge is required. It is nothing more than logs fashioned into a tiny home."

She recalled Shoomis telling her Great-Grandfather had trapped in a similar fashion—constructing small log homes on his trapline.

"Are winters always this bad?"

He shrugged. "The animals warn us in the fall of what to expect, but other times Winter Maker plays tricks, as he did this year. He not only surprised us, he surprised the creatures of the forest. I was lucky and found two frozen rabbits. There was not much meat on them. They'd starved to death, but I was able to eat. I gave your father and grandfather my ration of pemmican. We spent days tracking, and finally found some. The deer must have been separated from the herd."

"We ate the rabbit I kept as a friend."

"A friend?" Amusement lurked in Charlot's voice. "Do you mean a pet like the king does?"

Fire Woman nodded.

"This did not upset you as the capture of the Sioux, did it?"

"No. I can understand how unpredictable the seasons are, especially winter. You do what you have to do to survive."

"Ah, you are becoming one of the People, hmm?" He withdrew his tinder of tobacco and pipe from his cup.

"I am. If I had any doubts of returning, they vanished after what I experienced." Fire Woman ate the last of the meat. She'd eaten cautiously. To eat until she was full might sicken her, Mother had warned. She sipped the water beside her.

Curiosity reflected in Charlot's eyes. "You really mean that, don't you?"

"Yes."

"Then I best set my sights elsewhere, hmm?" He chuckled and picked up his tin of tea.

"What do you mean?" She set aside her water.

"I assumed you would divorce your husband and return east. Divorce is quite common among your people." He lit the pipe.

Divorce was also too common in the twenty-first century. "There will be no divorce. I will never leave Thunder Bear. Ever."

Any lingering doubts of returning home to her real family were done. She was Fire Woman, and *Gitche Manidoo* had created her to be Thunder Bear's wife, and to live with her true People.

Her first winter had been brutal, as if testing her resilience, and she had passed. She could face many more winters of hardship, because this was simply the way of life out here.

Chapter Eighteen: True Believer

The camp had moved again, and the sight of the dome-shaped lodges warmed Fire Woman's insides. When she feasted her gaze on Song Sparrow, delight jumped in her heart. She ignored the toboggan her husband pulled and hiked as fast as she could to her best friend.

"You! You!" Song Sparrow cried out. "I hear you are married now."

Fire Woman wrapped her arms around Song Sparrow, taking in the fresh scent of nature on her beloved *Anishinaabe* sister. "Yes, I am. How I missed you."

"I missed you, too." Song Sparrow held just as tightly as Fire Woman did. "It was such a rough winter. So rough. We lost Grandfather."

"Oh, I am so sorry." Fire Woman palmed Song Sparrow's cheeks. "When did this happen?"

"During the storm. Our food rations depleted. He told us to eat his share. Then he wandered off into the blizzard. We never saw him again." Sadness crept into Song Sparrow's gaze.

Fire Woman again hugged her dear friend, for she'd heard of the older people giving up their lives so the younger ones could live. "I am sure he walks in the spirit world now."

Song Sparrow laid her head on Fire Woman's shoulder. "I miss him very much. He will never see me marry or see my children."

"You are thinking of marrying?" Fire Woman again laid her hands on Song Sparrow's face.

"Not yet, but I will one day. I have set my sights on our French friend." Touching the mitten, Song Sparrow eyed Fire Woman. "These are beautiful. Did you make them?"

"Yes. Mother was very proud of my project. I am becoming more skilled with my sewing. I had all winter to practice." The rabbit fur in the lining was pure toasty warmth on Fire Woman's hands, courtesy of White One. She'd never forget the beloved rabbit.

"These are very pretty." Song Sparrow caressed the rabbit's feet tied to the ends of Fire Woman's braids.

"They are from my special friend. He came to me during my . . ." Heat claimed Fire Woman's face, for everyone must have heard. At least Song Sparrow hadn't shunned her. " . . . my banishment."

"But you are with your family again. I see your husband smiling and looking our way. All is well?"

"Very well." A grin stretched Fire Woman's lips. "I can hardly wait to learn how to tap the maple trees." Something Shoomis and Koko had done with their parents. "I must first ready the lodge and get the cache Mother and I stored during the fall. By the way, you said you have set your sights on the Frenchman. Did you mean Charlot?"

Song Sparrow mischievously grinned. "He likes the ladies. He always warms a woman's furs. Two summers ago, he tried to warm mine. As tempted as I was, I told him no."

Fire Woman blinked. "Goodness, he does . . . seem to leap from one sleeping robe to the next."

"I am going to tell him he can share my robe, but he must stay the full night, or he cannot." Song Sparrow set her hands on her hips.

Charlot settle down? Fire Woman glanced at her friend. "You understand he will eventually return to the land of the rising sun."

"No. He will stay here. Of that, I am sure." A twinkle

glimmered in Song Sparrow's eyes. "His heart is here." Just then Song Sparrow's mother called to her. "I must go. I will come see you tonight. We can talk more then."

"I will make you something to eat." Fire Woman pecked her friend's cheek. "Bring an empty belly."

"I will."

Fire Woman spent the rest of the day readying their new home among the maple trees, where they would stay until they moved to their summer camp. Straight into the evening, she aided Mother with unpacking the cache, covering the wigwam from the stored birch, unloading the toboggan, setting up the interior of the lodge, gathering firewood, and starting a meal. Her husband had gone fishing to spear some trout she could smoke.

They had also entered the small supply shack that had been built ages ago and removed everything carefully stored from the last season Fire Woman had not been a part of. Flutters again resided in her stomach. Lately, her belly was always dancing.

She slapped her hand over her mouth. Her moon time. She had not experienced one during the Snowcrust Moon. Would she bleed during the Sugarbushing Moon?

"What is it, daughter?" Mother glanced up from the fire pit where meat boiled in the big pot.

"I . . . I . . ."

"Have not visited the women's lodge?" Mother straightened.

Heat stung Fire Woman's cheeks. Thunder Bear had returned at the very beginning of the Snowcrust Moon. Naturally, they'd stolen under the robes to enjoy his homecoming. In the twenty-first century, she knew her menstrual cycle by looking at the calendar, but out here, she had nothing to gauge the days. Only months. But there was a good chance she'd been experiencing ovulation when they had come together as one.

"I guess I will know if I do not have to visit the lodge this moon." She couldn't help the shyness and pleasure in her voice.

"Daughter, I hope you do not have to visit it, either." Mother came up and hugged Fire Woman. "We need more children in our camp. Many more children."

"I hope to have many." In the twenty-first century, most had two children and waited until their late twenties or early thirties. For some women, even their forties. Out here, though, Fire Woman would birth as many as *Gitche Manidoo* saw fit, for she knew her husband would be a good provider for their expanding family.

"What about you?" Fire Woman peeked at her mother's stomach. "Is there anything resting in you?"

"No . . ." Mother sadly shook her head. "You know I visited the lodge. But I will keep hoping."

"I hope so, too. Imagine if we both carried children together." She laced her fingers with Mother's hands, rough from hard work, matching Fire Woman's calloused palms. "You are still young. Only thirty-five summers."

They would honor the second anniversary of her parents' loss this spring. Sixteen was too young to die. She wished she'd known her dead sister.

"This is no time for sadness." Mother slid her finger beneath Fire Woman's chin and coaxed her head up. "This is a time of rebirth. A time to celebrate. A time to visit."

"I invited Song Sparrow to join us for the evening meal. I missed her greatly."

"See?" Mother arched her brow. "It is a time of good."

A time of good was right. The birch bark baskets hung from the stand of trees where Mother and Father harvested the maple sap. Some of the bigger trees had two or three taps while the smaller trees had one.

Over the winter, Thunder Bear had traded his furs for a big pot to hang above the fire to boil the sap. He'd also collected plenty of wood for the women, while Swift Deer and Kicking Elk speared fish from the nearby stream. Another rack had been set up for drying the fish. Fire Woman could finally appreciate the eyes of the fish as a delicacy. Her stomach no longer came close to tossing up the morsel she'd force herself to eat.

They would remain here until the end of the Sugarbush Moon and what was known as *the last run*, when the trees let out their final gasp of very thick sap.

In the evenings, Fire Woman worked on cloth skirts for herself. Thunder Bear had also returned home with bolts of fabric. She shivered, because she'd seen sketches of *Anishinaabe-kweg* in such clothing in the early eighteen hundreds. History was rolling along just as the books had predicted.

The fire crackled and burned. She added another log and picked up the latest creation she was working on. The deerskin proved much thicker and warmer, but the leggings beneath her cloth skirt kept her legs warm whenever she was outside. She was working on the sleeves to Thunder Bear's soon-to-be shirt.

The flap to the wigwam moved. Her husband entered. He sat beside her and laid his palm on her bent legs. "You have not visited the women's lodge . . . again."

Fire Woman gazed at him. In a soft voice, she said, "No. I do believe I should have by now."

He moved his hand upward and rested his palm on her womb. "What do you think?"

"It is too soon to tell. But if I don't visit the lodge during the next moon . . ." Excitement fluttered in her heart.

"You have not visited it twice. I like to believe our child sleeps in your belly." His whispered words were hot steam on her ear.

"I hope you are right." Leaning her head on his shoulder where she always received comfort was not possible at the moment because public displays of affection were not allowed with her parents sitting across from them.

Father was tightening his bow, and Mother was stitching a shirt.

"I am right, wife. I am more than right," Thunder Bear murmured.

One evening they went to Thunder Bear's older brother's lodge. Raincloud stood at the entrance to greet them. He was as handsome as Fire Woman's husband.

"Brother, you have not officially met my wife. Greet your new sister, Fire Woman. Wife, this is your brother, *Gimiwa-naanakwad*, Raincloud."

Fire Woman offered her new relation a humble smile.

Raincloud's gaze moved up and down. The straight line of his red lips formed into a smile. "Welcome, sister. It is good to officially meet you."

Fire Woman met the rest of his in-laws, since her brother-in-law resided with his wife's family. While they ate and talked, she held Little Beaver in her arms, Raincloud's firstborn son after having two daughters. She drew her finger along the sleeping baby's protruding lower lip.

"How old is he?" she asked First Light of the Rising Sun, Raincloud's wife.

"He has seen two months." First Light of the Rising Sun cuddled When the Moon Hides on her lap, her youngest daughter, of three summers.

The child poked at her mother's breast, obviously wanting milk.

Fire Woman giggled. "She will not leave the nourishment alone, will she?"

"She is jealous." The black irises of First Light of the Rising Sun's eyes shone. "She loves the new baby, but she is not ready to relinquish her place as my youngest."

"How about your other daughter?" Fire Woman pursed her lips in the direction of Dawn is Breaking, the eldest child of Raincloud, who sat by her grandmother.

"She is very proud and believes she's Little Beaver's second mother." First Light of the Rising Sun shook her head, still smiling. "For only seeing five summers, she is mature beyond her years."

From her youthful beauty, Fire Woman assumed her sister-in-law had only seen maybe twenty-three summers. Her belly fluttered again. She might be getting a later start than most women in the camp, but soon she'd have her own brood of children to tend to and cherish.

"I am happy my brother found someone to love. I knew he was waiting for someone, but I did not realize he was waiting for you to arrive." First Light of the Rising Sun seemed to surmise more to herself. "I am happy you enjoy being with us. There is a glow to your face, a shine to your hair, and radiance in your eyes that speaks of a woman truly content."

"I am very content." Fire Woman slid her finger between the baby's lips, who suckled. "I have never known such happiness being a part of a . . ." Yes, it was more than her new family and husband swelling her heart. It was being in the circle of the community, of life. "Let us say I have found my place — where I truly belong."

The harvesting from the maple trees was a long but tedious and fun process. When the sap was collected from the trees, it was poured into the big boiling kettle that required constant stirring and the fire forever restocked.

The sugar was made into two types. First, before it granulated, the thick syrup for hard sugar had to be scooped from the big pot and dumped on the snow to harden. Once the sugar had firmed, Fire Woman had to pack it into birchbark cones. Then she sewed the cones shut with basswood fiber for storage. She also made sugar cakes into different shapes from wooden molds Father loved carving. Bear grease was lightly dusted into the molds so the sugar did not stick.

For the second type, she had to drop small pieces of deer tallow into the pot during the boiling stage. Again, when the sugar was about to granulate, she poured the contents of the big tub into a wooden trough Father had fashioned from a log he had smoothed-out. She had to stir the contents in the log. After the sugar had granulated, Mother stepped in with her ladles to rub the sugar down into grains. Then the still-warm sugar was poured from the trough into *makuks* of birchbark to be used for basic seasoning for their food, water, and the drying of berries.

Besides sugaring, the men kept the women busy with drying fish on the rack set up, and tending to the fire. Once hard, the fish were then packed away to be kept on hand for a quick morning meal.

Walleye was a different process, and not filleted the way Fire Woman was used to during a shore lunch. First, she had to clean and cut the fish along each side of the backbone, leaving the head attached. Then she hung each one over the top rails of the rack with the body on one side and the backbone and tail on the other. When the fish were almost dry, she had to split them lengthwise into thinner strips, and expose the insides to the fire.

She could not get over how much she was learning. By the time the year was up and she finally got to share a wigwam with her husband, she'd be self-sufficient, more than capable of tending to each task required of her.

If only her real family could see how she was flourishing. Shoomis and Koko would be proud. As for Mom, she'd probably shake her head and sigh, always having wanted *Edie* to accept the timeline she was born in to.

Her real parents would never see their first grandchild. A part of her heart wept, but she shrugged off the melancholy, for she desired to be nowhere else but here.

At the end of the moon, the camp was ready to leave for their summer residence. More work was required, from cleaning and storing the lot for the following year to making any necessary repairs to the equipment, lodges, and birch bark coverings.

Finally, everything was packed into their canoes. They were ready to leave. The ice had fully melted. She dipped her paddle into the water and started off in the very canoe owned by her husband, who steered. He said once they reached the camp, he'd fashion her a canoe, since the best time to harvest the precious bark was late spring and early summer, when it peeled easily off the birch tree in one piece.

Home was *Pikwedina Sagainan,* where she'd first met her ancestors and had been introduced to the true way of living. During their paddle, she didn't struggle. New muscles were in her arms that were stronger from her constant work over the months she'd resided with them.

Her heart bloomed at finally becoming a true *Anishinaabe-kwe,* just like Koko, and living the traditional life with her husband, who'd shown her patience, understanding, and sternness when needed.

"Wife, if you glow any brighter, you will blind me," he called out from the stern of the canoe.

"I am glowing?" She glanced over her shoulder to his strong arms steering the water vessel, sitting with his calves tucked beneath his thighs, and shoulders straight. His braided hair elongated his strong nose and sharpened his already sharp cheekbones.

"Yes, you are."

The birds chirping, the dipping of paddles into the water, and the peaceful sounds of nature were the most beautiful music she'd ever heard. "That is because I am happy. I was born for this."

His grin stretched to his ears. "Yes, I know this. I told you—*Gitche Manidoo* willed this to happen. You were destined to be my wife."

"Being your wife has made me the happiest woman on Turtle Island. The happiest woman who has ever lived." She faced the water again. "I can hardly wait until we have our own lodge."

"Patience. We will. And our home will be filled with many children."

She patted her tummy. Hopefully, a baby slept in her womb, and she would not have to visit the women's lodge during her expected moon time.

CHAPTER NINETEEN: WAR

Fire Woman hadn't suffered morning sickness. That had been taken care of by sipping the herb-laced tea Mother gave her each dawn upon waking. A pretty bump she was forever setting her hand on poked out from her skirt. Even Thunder Bear tended to lean over while they ate and touched her tummy where their child slept.

It was *Abitaa-niibini-giizis*, the halfway summer moon. Her garden was already planted. Berry picking was high on her chore list.

One evening, with her husband, they'd snuck off to the place where they'd met. Thunder Bear had plucked plenty of buttercups to gift her with to celebrate their union. While standing amongst the spruce trees and rocks, they'd gazed at where the flames had once flickered and danced, but none were present during their time alone together, something Fire Woman was grateful for, because she had no desire to return.

Part of her still worried for her real family and the pain they must be experiencing at her disappearance. Still, this was her true life now. Not the romantic dream she'd thought of as a young girl. This was hard work and much love.

She carried her basket of berries from the canoe her husband had built for her, having come from one of the many islands with the other women.

Drying her harvest wasn't hard work, either. Mother had shown Fire Woman the process of spreading field grass over the drying frame, which allowed the heat and smoke from the fire to creep through the grass and reach the berries. Once the berries were dried, she stored them in cedar bark woven pouches. Come the Ricing Moon, they'd add the wild rice to the pouches for a ready to boil winter meal with the sugar they'd stored during the Sugaring Moon.

"I will see you later," she said to Song Sparrow, who'd accompanied her. "Our friend is here. I am sure you wish to visit him."

"Indeed." Song Sparrow giggled.

Their gazes traveled to where Charlot stood.

"Go," Fire Woman urged her. "Enjoy yourself. We can talk come the next morning."

"I will more than enjoy myself. See you in the morning." Song Sparrow let out another giggle and hurried off.

Fire Woman approached Mother, who was at the drying rack, already working on the first batch of berries.

She set the big containers of birch bark down. "Here is some more."

"Plentiful." Mother's graceful, long fingers glided through the berries. "You are doing well, daughter. When the time comes for a lodge of your own, you will be more than capable of running it."

Pride swelled inside Fire Woman's chest. She knelt beside her mother. "Let me help. I won't go back until early morning to gather more. Song Sparrow is accompanying me."

Mother wiped her brow. "Fix us some sweetened water. I am thirsty."

Fire Woman's tongue also begged for a taste of the refreshing liquid. She poured them each a cup from the container where they stored water to keep nearby instead of having to always make trips to the lake. She added each a dash of maple sugar.

The men had gone off to fish. Soon, they would gather again for the *Midewiwin*. To see all the relations from Rainy Lake to Black Sturgeon Lake aroused flutters in Fire Woman's belly. Or maybe her child was awake. She set her hand on her stomach.

"Does the babe move?" Mother sipped from the cup. "I thought it was too early."

"It is me. I am looking forward to seeing everyone again at the fort."

"I am so proud of you." Mother reached out and toyed with the rabbit foot tied to Fire Woman's braid. "I will admit that after you let the Sioux free, I was not sure you would be able to live as we do, that the white man's society had stripped you of your true culture, but look at you now. A true *Anishinaabe-kwe*."

"I have no desire to return. You are my family." Fire Woman swept her hand across the air. "This place is my true home. And you are my mother." She arched her brow. "Is there something you are not telling me?"

"What would that be?" Mother puckered her lips.

"You have not visited the women's lodge in two moons now . . ."

Mother held her finger to her mouth. "Do not say anything, for I fear if I speak about what I hope is a baby growing in me, the child will fail to form."

"Then it's true?" Fire Woman gasped. She set aside her cup and reached over. The hug she lavished on Mother was one of joy and super tight. "It is true, isn't it? We are both carrying babies. Our children will grow up together."

"Daughter. Daughter." Woman of the Sky patted Fire Woman's back. "Remember, I am getting older. Moon cycles can change . . ."

"No. Not yet. It is too soon for your cycle to change. I know you are with child. Does Father know?"

"Of course not. I told you—I feared if I spoke too soon, I might—"

"I know you are carrying a child." Fire Woman kept

gripping her mother's waist. "This is meant to be. Our children are to grow up together. We are to raise them together."

Fire Woman rested in Thunder Bear's arms. For some reason she had woken, which was strange, for they had not retired until well into the night, staying awake to enjoy one another's flesh. Maybe it was the birdcalls. They seemed to come from different directions, as if the feathered beings had surrounded the village from the north, south, east, and west.

She peeked her head up. *Stop being silly.* There was nothing to fear. Scouts were out, the men taking turns watching over the camp. And just before the first peek of light, the birds chirped.

Thunder Bear set his hand very gently over her mouth. "I have heard them, too, wife. I am going to check in with the scouts."

She stiffened. "What does this mean?" Her words were muffled from his palm on her lips.

Thunder Bear sat up. "Dress. Very quietly. Then wake your mother and father."

While Thunder Bear donned his clothing, goosepimples broke out on Fire Woman's skin. She grabbed for the first clothing available. When Thunder Bear retrieved his musket and ammunition pouch, sorrow and terror infiltrated her heart.

"Is it the Sioux?" She grasped the fringes on his legging.

He glanced down at her, shaking his head at the cotton skirt she'd retrieved. "Make sure to wear your leggings, deerskin dress, and blanket. Braid your hair. Follow what your father says once I speak to him. He will aid you."

"Thunder Bear—"

He shook his head, meaning he was asking for her silence.

Fire Woman clamped her mouth shut, but as she looked to her parents, fright crept through her veins. She squeezed her eyes shut. She was living in a time of war. Battles were a part of their lives. Even ambushes. *Massacre Island*. She shivered — so many men had been slaughtered at the hands of the Dakota.

Quickly, she dressed in the proper clothing as instructed by her husband.

The flap to the wigwam opened. Charlot stepped inside. His grim gaze said something was terribly wrong.

"I know." Thunder Bear cradled his musket.

Mother and Father stirred. They both sat up.

"Let me go to the lodges of Kicking Elk and Swift Deer to wake them and their families. I will be right back." Thunder Bear ducked from the wigwam, still clutching his musket.

Fire Woman draped the blanket around herself. She wasn't cold, but she had to do something to stop the big ball of fear lodged in her throat, threatening to choke her.

Mother and Father dressed. Father reached for his musket — one of the biggest reasons the Ojibway had allied with the French, and why her husband trapped all late fall and into the winter for furs to trade.

Fire Woman refused to think about the safety of the home she'd left behind. War was going to happen between the Dakota and Ojibway for another hundred years, and their battles were as much a part of her life as the moccasins she'd donned and the rabbit feet wrapped around the deer strips to fasten her braids.

Walks with a Limp ducked from the wigwam.

Charlot stepped forward, but Thunder Bear reentered. He set his free hand on Charlot's shoulder. "This is not your battle to fight, my friend. Guard my wife. She must live. This is most important."

"*Oui.*" Charlot nodded. "As you request."

Thunder Bear leaned in and said something Fire Woman could not hear. Then he glanced to her. Love and courage shone in his eyes. "I will see you again, wife. Believe this, for I have kept every promise to you."

Before Fire Woman could reply, he again ducked from the wigwam.

"Come. We must get to where I was lodging. My musket is there." Charlot took Fire Woman's hand and led her from the wigwam.

Fire Woman glanced over her shoulder at her mother heading for the wigwam of the grandparents'. The word *Mother* sat on her lips, but Fire Woman did not dare yell. Everything was happening quietly, and the silence hanging in the air was like the moisture in the atmosphere before the arrival of a vicious thunderstorm.

Other people were sneaking from their wigwams, men with their bows and arrows or muskets. The Dakota were out there somewhere. They were the ones making the birdcalls.

She stood outside the wigwam where Charlot had entered to get his musket.

A shot rang out. The most bloodcurdling howl Fire Woman had ever heard in her life stood the hairs on the back of her neck and sent a spasm of fear down her spine. Charlot appeared and raced them into the bush. He cradled the butt of the musket in the crook of his arm.

"Run. Run fast," he urged her.

Screams echoed through the air. More war whoops followed. Then the loud blasts from the muskets joined in on the once peaceful early morning. Dawn was beginning to break. There wasn't enough light to see, but Charlot kept them moving at full speed, not once looking back.

He gripped her hand so tight, what nails he had dug into her palm.

Twigs whipped Fire Woman's face. She didn't have time to wince from the scratches. Her heart seemed to be beating in her throat, and her lungs threatened to explode from the rush of air moving along her windpipe.

In the darkness, a sense of déjà vu draped her in its suspicion. There was something familiar about their trek. Wait. She had made this journey twice now with Thunder Bear, even though their jaunts had happened during the day. Charlot was taking her to where she'd first stepped from the portal. Her mind rolled back to her husband's hushed words to Charlot inside the wigwam, and how Thunder Bear had also wanted to speak to her father.

Charlot was moving them so fast, she couldn't throw on her brakes to stop them, but she finally managed to dig her heels into the earth.

"What are you doing?" Charlot craned his neck.

"I . . . I know where you are taking me. I will not go back." She gritted her teeth.

"I am only following the instructions of your husband. He said for me to take you there, for your safety will be guaranteed. He said it is imperative you live. Now come. Do not argue. Obey the words of your husband."

"I will not go on without him." Fire Woman raised her chin.

"He has ordered you to follow my direction." Charlot's jawline stiffened in the shadows of the early morning. "Now obey as a good wife of a warrior should."

A lump built in Fire Woman's throat. Thunder Bear would not ask this of her unless he knew what the outcome could possibly be on their village. For all she knew, the Dakota could have arrived in huge numbers. *Massacre Island* rolled in front of her eyes.

"When were the men massacred? The French explorers— Jean Baptiste LaVerendrye, Father Aulneau, and the nineteen other men?"

Charlot peered. Suspicion was apparent in his questioning gaze. "Eight years ago."

Finally, Fire Woman had a time and year. It was the summer of seventeen forty-four. "We can go. I will wait there for my husband."

He nodded and rushed them through the thick bush of tall spruce trees and heavy underbrush. The smell of sap and wildflowers was calming to Fire Woman's shot nerves. Her teeth never stopped clacking during their journey to the place where she'd first met Thunder Bear.

Thank goodness she'd donned the appropriate outfit as directed by her husband. The deerskin, leggings, and blanket kept the rest of her skin from being scratched. Her braids stopped her hair from becoming tangled or flying about during their long running journey.

Charlot slowed and glanced around, as if trying to find a particular spot.

The echoes of shrieks, gunfire, and howls trailed them, spooking along Fire Woman's spine. Her breaths still came fast. Charlot was ushering them through the brush at top speed again.

A howl too close for comfort roared from the trees. The painted brave dropped out from a branch, clutching a tomahawk. Charlot released Fire Woman's hand. He cocked the musket, having most likely already loaded it, and squeezed the trigger. A loud blast almost tore off Fire Woman's ears — she'd already scrunched down, eyes shut tight and ears covered. The stench of gunpowder invaded her nostrils.

Her lids flickered. She glanced at Charlot, who laid his musket parallel. He opened the pan, then reached inside his pouch on his hip held by a strap draped across his chest. She gazed at the wadding he produced. He bit off part of the cartridge with his teeth and poured a portion of the powder into the pan.

During this, the Dakota lay on the ground, eyes staring wide, his chest open where blood pooled through his breast plate, mouth half open.

Charlot set the butt of the musket on the ground and poured the rest of the powder down the barrel. He released the ramrod and slid it into the barrel to keep the powder and ball from falling out. Three times he performed packing the powder. Then he recovered the ramrod. He halfcocked the hammer.

"Let's go." He took her hand again.

Fire Woman shimmied along behind him. More twigs and branches slapped her face. She clutched the blanket tightly with her other hand. The longer they ran, the more the gunshots, screams, and howls from the village faded on the light breeze skimming the top of the trees. There was also a new sound, though — war in the bush. No screams. Only whoops and gunfire.

"What are we going to do?" The words came out heavy and stuttered from her gasps for breaths.

"I am doing what your husband instructed me to do." Charlot kept them running.

By now, Fire Woman's thighs burned. Dawn had fully lit the sky. Soon the sun would rise. They never stopped running until they came across the rocks, thick underbrush of buttercups, and towering spruce trees.

Panting, Charlot stopped.

Fire Woman could not rip her gaze from the spot where she had first spied Thunder Bear. The gunfire and whooping had followed them. Somewhere, not far away, her husband must be fighting for his life, and there was nothing she could do to help him.

He would also not come for her. His first duty was to the People. Protect the community. Just as her first duty as an *Anishinaabe-kwe* was *mitakuye-oyasin* – all her relations suffering right now, which was why she'd run. The women and children had had to run, for if they did not, they would experience loss of life, and life was precious out here in the wilds. To lose too many in death meant having to restart the cycle again with more births and children to rear.

Charlot cradled the butt of the musket in his armpit. He laid his free hand over Fire Woman's face. His heavy breaths were steamy along her cheeks, and his green eyes searched hers. "If not for my loyalty to your people and all that they have done for my father and I to survive out here, I would have taken another path instead of bringing you to this unsafe place and kept you forever, *ma chérie*."

Dread dribbled down Fire Woman's spine. "What is that supposed to mean?"

"The Sioux came with the intent to massacre. Their numbers are far too great. Before we spirited into the woods, I saw the silhouette of their war canoes on the lake. They are everywhere."

Fear hugged her. "I'm going back for him—"

"You cannot. He asked me to bring you here to see you safely through these dancing flames he insisted will appear." Charlot spoke in a hushed voice. His gaze continued to search her face. "He cannot come for you. He must stay and see that the women and children are safely away from the attack. You know by staying he will not be returning. The birdcalls I heard this morning said the Sioux come from all directions. We are lucky we made it out alive, for many will not."

"I'm going back for him. I do not care if you accompany me or not." Fire Woman thrust her chin at him.

A whirring sound came through the air.

"I cannot let you ret—" Charlot's eyes popped to the size of birch bark baskets. He clutched the arrow embedded in his side.

Fire Woman screamed. Dakota braves seemed to appear out of the spruce trees. One had his arrow raised straight at her. She squeezed her eyes shut, waiting for the death blow.

Nothing happened. The only noise was Charlot's heavy breathing and slight groan.

He leaned on her.

She forced her eyes open. The Sioux were pointing and gasping at something behind her. She turned on her heel. The portal had appeared. Flames danced and shimmered.

"Go," Charlot gasped. "Go now."

Fire Woman clutched him. "They are afraid. They will not harm us."

"I said go. More are coming. You will not survive." Blood leaked from his side, which he continued to clutch. "Go now." He staggered slightly and lifted his musket at the Dakota, who continued to gape at the portal.

"I will not leave you to fight this battle by yourself. You are my friend —"

Charlot used his foot to shove her rear end. Fire Woman screamed and staggered forward, straight into the portal.

CHAPTER TWENTY: UNIVERSAL YOU

Edie stumbled forward. Grass came at her. Grass she knew from over a year ago. War cries followed, slicing into her ears. She threw out her hands and landed face-first on the ground. Heart pounding, she whipped her head. Charlot fired his musket. He hit his target of a Sioux brave, just as the other braves raised their bows and arrows. The dancing flames were vanishing, and so were Charlot and the Dakota.

The portal was closing. She stood and rushed at it. "Charlot!" she cried out. "No!"

Instead of managing to break through to the other side to help her dear French friend, she hit the thick wall of corn.

She slammed her fist against it. "Thunder Bear," she cried out. Panic rose inside her. She'd spoken in English. This couldn't be happening. There had to be a way to get back.

The scarecrow.

She dashed through the maze, clutching her blanket tightly around her. When she popped outside, the candles in the pumpkins continued to flicker and burn. She launched her gaze at the moon. It was the same night. Halloween. But there was no scarecrow at the entrance.

Somehow, she had to find another portal. She whirled around on her heel. Before her, the corn maze began to fade.

"No!" she hollered.

She sprang forward, but she didn't enter the maze. The labyrinth had vanished. She stood in an open field under the light of the moon.

"Thunder Bear," she again cried out. "Thunder Bear."

No sound came from anywhere. Not even a rustle of wind.

With agony burrowed in her heart, she sank to the ground. The wail came deep from her chest and exploded from her mouth. Tears rained from her eyes. The lump in her throat was unbearable and seemed to burn her windpipe. She rocked back and forth. What she'd experienced couldn't have been a dream. Her heart was in tatters, mourning the loss of her husband and family, of the People she'd come to cherish.

Never again would she see Thunder Bear, her parents, Song Sparrow, or Charlot. They couldn't live merely in her imagination. They were true memories.

She set her hand on her belly where her bump resided. Somehow, she had gone back in time, because Thunder Bear's child remained in her womb. "Oh please, *Mandaamin*, pity me. Return me to where I truly belong."

More silence greeted her.

On quivering legs, she rose to her feet, still clutching the blanket tightly around her. The car she'd parked remained in its spot. She hobbled to the vehicle, swiping at her tears.

Had they lived? Had they died? What had happened to her husband, family, best friend, and Charlot? If she didn't return, she'd have no choice but to go home and have the baby. What would her parents say, her brothers, her sister, Shoomis, and Koko?

"Please," she again begged, looking to the midnight-blue sky. "Please, *Mandaamin*, hear me. Return me to where I belong."

A deflated tire on her car greeted her.

She fisted her hands and set them against her temples. The frustrated scream shot from between her lips. She kicked the flat. A burning sensation dug into her toes, since she only had on moccasins. She smacked her hand over her mouth and held her hurting foot.

This was too much to endure. She flopped on the fallen

blanket, drew her knees to her chest, and cuddled herself.

The recognizable sporting roar from the motorcycle engine she'd heard the night she'd gone into the portal carried to where she sat with tears still streaming from her eyes. The logical part of her said to run to the road and wave for help, but the other part that bore deep wounds in her heart remained seated. She never bothered swiping at her tears. Horrible sobs kept coming from her mouth.

The bike slowed, which was strange, because he'd have had to flash his light in the direction of where she sat to see her. Maybe his high beam had caught some kind of reflection from her car.

He turned the bike. The high beam came straight in her direction, forcing Edie to squeeze her lids shut and hold up her hand to spare her pupils from the bright glare.

A hint of anger crept into her chest. After what she'd endured, she wasn't ready to see anyone. Her heart was continuing to cry for her husband, who she'd never cherish again unless she found another way to return.

The bike came to a halt about ten feet from her. The man lifted his long leg from the frame. His perfect V build was buried beneath a leather jacket. The chaps hugging his legs defined his firm-looking thighs. He set his hands on the helmet and pulled. Slowly, the black apparatus slid off his head to reveal one-length jet-black hair grazing his strong shoulders.

When he bared his face of a long and sharp nose, narrow eyes that matched the hue of his hair, cheekbones capable of cutting diamonds sitting high on his oblong face, and slim lips the shade of poppies, Edie's heart stopped pattering.

On quivering legs, she struggled to stand. She grabbed the blanket beneath her. No, it could not be . . .

Yet Thunder Bear's departing declaration to her before he'd left the wigwam blinked on and off in her mind . . . *I will see you again, wife. Believe this, for I have kept every promise to you.*

The same questioning look Thunder Bear had given Edie

on the day she'd first encountered him was in the squint of the man's gaze. His stare traveled from her moccasins to her two braids.

The man cleared his throat, but his eyes remained in a squint. "Do you . . . do you need help?"

Edie's hope fell to her feet. The man might possess Thunder Bear's voice, handsome face, and glorious body, but her husband had never hesitated or stuttered. "I am fine." She raised her chin.

The man glanced at her flat tire. "Are you sure?"

Thunder Bear would have taken control, telling her he was changing the tire. "Yes, I am fine. I have roadside assistance. I will call them."

The man set his hands on his slim hips. "You know as well as I do how long it takes roadside assistance to reach anyone in the boondocks. I should know. I'm from a rez in Manitoba."

"What brings you far from your motherland?" She glanced away. Her peripheral vision caught the curiosity flecking his gaze. He was studying her again.

"You speak rather formally."

"I do not know what you mean."

"I got a buddy from here. He invited me down for the weekend. He said there was . . . well, a Halloween party happening. He mentioned I should meet someone." He moved his hand up and down. "Were you on your way to the party?"

What an insult. Anyone with a brain could tell she was wearing a traditional dress and moccasins. "Do I look like I am wearing a costume?" She didn't mean to snap, but her grief was too great.

"Nope. You look like you came through time. Except for one thing—your features. You know as well as I do, we allied with the French when they first came here, and they married a lot of our women."

Charlot. He'd probably sacrificed his life to save her. "Yes, they did. And they were good men."

"Let me change your tire. I have a story to tell you." He removed his leather jacket to reveal a bear claw necklace. Not just any bear claw necklace. Thunder Bear's necklace.

Edie gasped and inched in closer. Sure enough, the one claw was fractured, as Thunder Bear had shown her.

"Pop your trunk."

"Um . . . y-yes." She stumbled to her car. "I-I just gotta . . . my keys are somewhere in here."

"So much for your formal speech, huh?" He chuckled.

Annoyance crept up Edie's back. "What's that supposed to mean?" She grabbed her keys and pressed the button to open the trunk.

"Engage your parking brake." He sauntered to the back of the car with a lazy gait.

He was taking charge—just as Thunder Bear had. Edie shivered and engaged the emergency brake. She shut the car door and rounded the vehicle. The man already had the trunk open and was rifling through it. He unpacked the kit Dad had gotten her when she'd first started university.

She stiffened. She hadn't thought *Father*, but *Dad*. No, she would not live like a twenty-first century person. She would not acclimatize to this time period, not when she belonged in the past.

The words of the *jaasakiid* floated across her brain. The man had predicted she'd come back to . . . to what? To learn the true way—the ways of her ancestors. The *jaasakiid* had told her she must return the knowledge she'd acquired to the present-day People.

The man removed the spare tire from the trunk. He also grabbed a flashlight. "Here. Hold this up so I can see what I'm doing."

Edie took the flashlight, but not before their fingers touched. The same electrical surge coursed through her veins

as when she'd first connected her flesh with Thunder Bear's —
the moment that had bound them together for eternity.

She snatched away her hand. "I . . . I don't even know your
name."

"Oh, I think you do." He moved around the car and squatted in front of the flat. "My English name is Adrian Moneas.
My Ojibway name is *Nimkii Makwa*."

Edie almost stomped her foot. Red heat spread across her
chest. This couldn't and wouldn't be true. Someone must be
playing a joke on her. There had to be an explanation . . ."You
said you come from a reserve in Manitoba."

"Yeah . . ." He kept glancing at her while removing the
hubcap. "My family migrated there a long time ago. We originally come from *Pikwedina Sagainan*."

"You're lying!" She couldn't help shouting. Hearing him
confirm what might possibly be true was an affront to the sac-
rifice Thunder Bear had made for her and the People. Now
here was this idiot trying to claim to be . . ."There is no way
in hell you are from here."

Just as Thunder Bear would, Adrian stopped loosening the
lug nuts, set the wrench on his strong thigh, and gazed at her
with the utmost patience in his dark eyes. "Why is that so
hard to believe, *Ishkode-kwe*?"

Holy hell, he knew her fucking name! She had to tighten
her grip on the flashlight before her shaking hands dropped
the damned thing. "All of this . . . it's a joke, right? Everyone
at the party is in on it!"

She shucked the flashlight and pivoted to the place where
the maze once was.

His straightening and setting aside the wrench carried on
the air to where she stood.

"*Ishkode-kwe*, look at me."

Her trembling body bordered on breaking apart at every
joint. She slowly turned her head to his understanding gaze.

"We are not to speak about our vision quests, but when my dad sent me on mine, it was revealed to me I would have to share what I learned with my dad and *Ishkode-kwe*." He pushed back his hair that had fallen forward, tucking the strands behind his ears.

Having his face on full display was going through the portal and first meeting Thunder Bear. Her head threatened to float above her if it became any lighter while her heart tugged for the man she'd lost that could possibly be standing in front of her.

He squatted again. "I told my dad what I saw in my vision. I saw . . . you, as you are now."

Edie kept trembling. She had picked up the flashlight and held tight to it again.

"My dad told me a story passed down to each firstborn son of my many greats grandfather *Gimiwanaanakwad*."

This was surreal. He spoke of Thunder Bear's elder brother?

"You see, when Raincloud's son, *Amikoonse*, was old enough, he shared the story and told his son to pass it on to his firstborn son. That it was imperative he repeat each word. Over generations, each son birthed first continued what Raincloud had started."

She squeezed her eyes shut. The day she'd met Little Beaver, he'd still been in the moss bag, a first son for Raincloud after two daughters.

"I'm the firstborn in my family and the firstborn son." He grabbed the jack and began to lift the vehicle. "I have a younger brother and sister."

"What did your father tell you?" Edie murmured. She moved in closer.

The car was fully jacked up. Adrian worked on the lug nuts he'd loosened, removing them one by one. "He told me about my many greats uncle and his death."

The sob Edie thought she'd disposed of reappeared in her throat. Thunder Bear was truly gone, either from the arrow of a Dakota or time passing. She glanced away.

"I'm named after him. It was the name given to me at my naming ceremony by an elder. The thing is, he had no clue who Thunder Bear was 'cause he never heard the story." Adrian gathered up the lug nuts and set them out of the way. "But it was the name he gave me after I had my vision quest."

Did Edie dare ask? She shuffled in even closer. "Your vision quest . . ."

"I told you already. I saw you." He used his chin to point at her. He glanced back at the vehicle. "I saw you the way you're dressed now. That's why I seemed a little freaked when I removed my helmet to get a good look at you."

Freaked? Thunder Bear would never use such a word. "I see . . ."

"I'm studying for my master's at the U of M. Political science."

"You want to become a politician?" The taste of the air was on Edie's tongue, a rich flavor of spruce and pine.

"Yep." He grunted. He held the tire in both hands that he'd removed from the hub. "My father, grandfather, great-grandfather, and my uncles all served in some capacity in politics. It's wired into me."

He set aside the tire and reached for the spare. "During my last year of high school, I lived with my aunt in the city. I'd gotten a job as a page at the Manitoba Legislative. It was pretty cool. Then I went for my BA in Ottawa, because I was selected as a page for the House of Commons."

Edie stiffened. "I see . . ."

"Y'know how it goes. If you wanna learn, you gotta check it out from every angle, not just what's familiar to you. I spent my formative years learning everything about Band Council at the local level on my rez. But I also needed to make connections and find out more about the Canadian govern-ment."

"So you are educated in Indigenous and Canadian poli-tics," Edie concluded.

Adrian nodded. He fitted the spare on the hub and patted the tire. "My goal is to become the MP of our riding back in Manitoba one day."

"You will remain in Manitoba?"

"Yep. My buddy said that's where you attend school. He said you're at the U of W."

"How does your friend know me?"

"Well, he wanted me to meet you, didn't he?" Adrian glanced up, his eyes twinkling. "That's why he invited me down for the weekend."

"Strange. My friend Tamara wanted me to meet some-one—"

"Tamara? Her last name wouldn't be Big George, would it?" Adrian had lowered the jack slightly until the tire brushed the ground.

"Yes, it is. Why?"

"That's who my buddy talked to. Arnold Wayash."

"Arnold?" Edie sputtered. She knew Arnold. He was at-tending the U of M and had grown up with Tamara.

Adrian tightened every other lug nut. Then he started on the alternating lug nuts he'd passed over during his first round. "Yeah, Arnold. He wanted to introduce me to . . . you."

Chapter Twenty-One: Be Free

"Me?" Edie set her hand on her chest.

"Yeah. He told me I ought to meet Edie. Edie White-crow." Adrian finished tightening the last lug. "A really smart girl, really beautiful, who's taking Indigenous Studies at the U of W. So he invited me down for the weekend."

"I see . . ." Edie glanced away. She rubbed the bump gifted to her by Thunder Bear. As attractive as Adrian was, and as much as the chemistry was literally exploding between them, he was not her husband. Her mourning time was one year, but she did not have her in-laws to reside with.

"I told you — she looked exactly like you in my vision. *That* and all."

"That?" Edie turned her head.

"Yeah, *that*." He used his chin to motion at her bump.

An armor of defensiveness encircled Edie. "It is a gift from my husband."

"I know about your husband. Thunder Bear." He fingered the bear claw necklace. "You know where this comes from, don't you?"

If Edie heard anymore from this man, the anger thrashing in her would burst into flames. How could Adrian be her long lost Thunder Bear? "My husband wore one."

"I know he did. He woke the bear during his first hunt. Much to Thunder Bear's regret, he had to kill his spirit brother."

Again, the lump swelled in Edie's throat.

"Maybe this will prove to you what happened." He stood.

Edie backed up one step. Apprehension beat in her heart.

He turned and lifted his t-shirt.

Much to Edie's shock—a shock that almost ripped her chest wide open—she gaped at the very same scar Thunder Bear had possessed from the bear's claws. The claws he'd taken for his necklace.

"I was told he'd live again." Adrian lowered his shirt. He set aside the wrench and took a step closer to her. His scent carried to Edie, the same scent of the outdoors and leather. "If you need more proof, my vision told me where I can find the plastic beads."

"Plastic. Plastic . . . beads?" The very ones Thunder Bear had picked from her dress on the first day they'd met?

"Yeah, the beads . . ."

Edie wet her lips. A chill shimmered along her backside. "That is not necessary. You may continue."

A light smile dusted Adrian's mouth. "Y'see, my dad said Thunder Bear, our many greats uncle, died during a Dakota attack. He died defending the woman and people he loved. He was with his elder brother, Raincloud. He told Raincloud not to mourn him, for he'd live again. He had to live again to care for the child and the wife who'd walked through the dancing flames."

"Oh my fucking God!" Edie spun on her moccasin. The sob launched itself from her throat.

"During my vision quest, fire burned in my gut. I swore I was dying. The pain was enormous," Adrian continued on. His tone had become melodic and soft, just like her husband's. "Something sharp had pierced me. It was deep in one of my organs. I knew something terrible was going to happen. And then I saw . . . you."

"M-me?" Edie squeaked out.

"Yeah, you." This time he actually pointed, which was considered taboo among their people, for shoving a finger in any direction was considered rude. "Just like I said, you look how you do now. You were calling to me. I knew you were grieving and trying to find me."

"And . . . and the Frenchman?" She inched in farther.

"He died. Raincloud found him at the site where Thunder Bear had instructed his brother to go before he passed away. Raincloud found the Frenchman riddled with arrows. I guess he died saving you. Thunder Bear had insisted you had to live. He never said why, other than the Thunderbirds had entrusted him with your safety."

Charlot had taken many arrows for her. She almost sagged to the ground.

"I am trying to find a way to go back," she whispered.

"Why?" He closed the gap between them. "You know what happened. It was a sneak attack. The few who survived left. Your mother. Your father. They knew the French explorers had gone on to Manitoba, and that was where our people fled to. They ended up settling on Lake Winnipeg, where my family lives now. There's nothing there to return to."

No, there wasn't.

He slid his finger under her chin in the way Thunder Bear used to do. "Look at me, *Ishkode-kwe*. It is I, *Nimkii Makwa*. There has been no other but you. I tried dating. I did. But my heart told me it had already been taken. When I first saw you, I knew I had finally come home."

"Home . . ." Edie croaked out. She laid her head on his shoulder. His scent and strength were the familiar essence she'd experienced numerous times in the past. "It is really you, husband?"

"Yes, wife, it is I." His words were steamy heat on her ear. "Did you really believe I'd abandon you? Did you really think I'd fail to protect you? I protected you in the only way I knew how — with my life. Now I am here to protect and love you again, just as I promised the night we were married. Just as

I'd promised when I left our lodge to fight the Dakota."

Oh God, he had kept his promise. He'd moved time. He'd moved centuries. He'd moved life to be here with her. "H-husband, it is really you." The sob in her throat reappeared.

"Yes, it is I." He cupped her face.

"Then take us back. Take us back to our People. Husband, I wish we could go back. I cannot bear to be without my mother, my father, your mother, your father . . . our families. Living with our ancestors in the true way was the happiest time I'd ever experienced." She nuzzled his shoulder. "It's all destroyed. Made into a country now. Ruled by a government. Culture ripped from us. An invisible line drawn down the great mass of water."

"You don't think people still live traditionally?" His words were softer than buttercups on her ear. His strong hand moved in a gentle circle on her lower back. "You were re-turned here to help the People. Why do you think you're studying what you are? Why do you think you weren't killed that morning of the attack? Why do you think I'm studying for my master's? We, as a People, are thriving again. We will keep thriving. Soon, we will be as strong as our ancestors once were."

"Is that why you wish to become an MP?" She lifted her head and gazed into his narrow eyes that glittered.

"I'm only twenty-four, but someday I will have the experi-ence to lead our riding. I've spent my teenage years working toward this."

"What about our baby? I am only in my second year of my studies." She touched his face.

In this day and age, they were both so young to be having a family.

He fingered her braid. "Wife, you are always worrying. Al-ways so full of fear. Did not *Gitche Manidoo* will this? Trust Him. We will be fine. You have learned the customs of

Anishinaabe-kweg. We will have the baby. When you wish, you can return to school and finish your education."

"There is not much else to learn after what I was taught by our ancestors," she admitted. "Education is life and experience, and I learned firsthand from my adoptive parents and family. Most of all, I learned from my husband. I experienced the *Midewiwin* and unearthed that being a doctor is more than medicine. It is also a curing of the spirit, the nourishment of one's soul to live the good life.

"That is all we wanted as a People—to live good and healthy lives. Is that not what we want in the present day, too?"

"Yes, we do." He nodded.

"Yet, we chase objects, things." She frowned. "I even chased objects and things before I visited our ancestors for one year." She touched his cheek again. "It is not objects, money, or things. It is love. Simply love. Serving the people you love. Helping the people you love. Providing for the people you love."

Her real family loved her.

A lightbulb seemed to explode in a flash of light in her head.

"Oh geez, husband!" For her entire life, she'd chased a dream when what she'd craved was in the twenty-first century—parents, grandparents, brothers, sister, friends, and a wonderful education waiting for her to help those in the here and now. Most of all, she had the love of Thunder Bear.

Shoomis would believe her tale once she told him what had happened and why she was pregnant.

The crooked smile on her husband's face was as if he was reading her mind and *tsking* her in a gentle but chiding way. "I am here to serve, help, and provide for you and our child, wife. And to serve, help, and provide for the People through my education." He kept stroking her braid.

"Then let's go home," she whispered.

"We'll go home." His knuckles were beneath her chin. He tilted her face up.

"First, you must meet my family." She gazed into his dark eyes.

"Of course I will. Is this not what a man does when he takes a wife? He lives with his wife's family for a full year."

"Your studies, though . . ." She wet her lips.

"We will seek guidance as we did in the old days—through our elders. Once we speak to your parents and grandparents, *Gitche Manidoo* will tell us what we are to do next."

Funny, Thunder Bear had always stressed that to her, and here he was, stressing those same words again.

His mouth came down on hers.

She was wrapped in the same magical kiss Thunder Bear had lavished on her in the past. He'd moved and shoved time for them to be together once again. She held tight, tasting his silky lips, marveling at the smooth muscles she touched beneath his t-shirt, and wondered at the sensual scent on his skin.

She broke the kiss. "I was so afraid I'd lost you."

"I'm here, *Ishkode-kwe*." He cupped her face. "This is where we're meant to be. This is what we were born for."

"Born for this?" She gazed up at him.

"Yep. Born for this time and place, to be together. Forever." His mouth claimed hers again.

You may also enjoy the following from eXtasy Books Inc:

Sanctified
Maggie Blackbird
September 20, 2019

In the midst of a battle for leadership at their Ojibway community, two enemies of opposing families fall in love . . .

After suffering a humiliating divorce, infuriated Catholic Jude Matawapit bolts to his family's Ojibway community to begin a new job—but finds himself thrown into a battle for chief as his brother-in-law's campaign manager. The radical Kabatay clan, with their extreme ideas about traditional Ojibway life, will stop at nothing to claim the leadership position and rid the reserve of Western culture and its religion once and for all, which threatens not only the non-traditional people of the community, but Jude's chance at a brand-new life he's creating for his children.

Recovering addict Raven Kabatay will do anything to win the respect and trust of her older siblings and mother after falling deep into drug addiction that brought shame and anger to her family. Not only does she have the opportunity to redeem herself by becoming her brother's campaign manager for chief—if he wins, she'll have the reserve's backing to purchase the gold-mine diner where she works, finally making something of herself. But falling in love with the family's sworn enemy—the deacon's eldest son, Jude—will not just betray the Kabatay clan. It could destroy everything Raven believes in and has worked so hard for.

Excerpt

Frost nipped at Raven's exposed skin, the kind of frost that burned. At least there wasn't a wind chill, or minus thirty-seven would become minus forty-seven. She scurried from her sister's truck she'd parked, dashed up the shoveled walkway, and into the school.

All was quiet, classes for the kids having finished for the day. The scent of pine cleaner permeated the squeaky-clean hallway. She hurried to the adult education classroom. Since her vehicle was the lone truck in the lot, she might be the only one here. Even the new principal wasn't present, unless he'd foolishly walked over.

She entered the classroom to Jude Matawapit sitting at the teacher's desk, hunched over, writing on some paper.

"I was beginning to wonder if any of my students would arrive." His strong fingers gripped a pen. His jet-black hair with blue undertones was slicked off his face and tapered to a short-trimmed back. Dark irises richer than a moonless night, so dark his lashes gave the illusion of a generous coating of mascara and liner-rimmed eyes, stared at her.

Not gawked, not ogled, not leered like every other guy did. He simply stared. His plump lips didn't form into a flirty smile, either.

Jude stood. A white dress shirt hugged his pumped biceps and shoulders that formed into the size of baseballs. A black belt wrapped his ultra-slim waist. And a gold clip kept his line-striped burgundy tie secure. "Have a seat. It looks to be you and me tonight."

Raven inched up the aisle. Her boldness remained at the door, where she'd probably dropped her tongue. She clutched her books and sat at the desk directly in front of him.

"I've been reviewing your file." He closed the folder, and just like Deacon Matawapit, crossed his strong arms. They even shared the same rich baritone — direct and full of authority. "You were an A-plus student, but as of late you haven't been handing in assignments. Once you get behind, it's difficult to catch up. I've seen this happen too many times during my years educating others. When a student falls behind, most give up."

A flame of annoyance flickered in Raven's stomach. Never mind Jude Matawapit's handsome white teeth, flawless red-toned brown skin, or run-her-nails-along-his-muscles build. Who was he to talk down to her like a kid? He was worse than her siblings and Mom.

Raven stared up at the white stucco ceiling. "I've been extremely busy. Not all of us make big money and do what we please. I've been pulling extra shifts at the diner."

"Did you review your last three assignments, then?" Jude stuck the end of the pen into his mouth.

There was something about the way his red lips and white teeth nibbled on the cap. And she hadn't witnessed a man in his late thirties gnawing on one like a hungry beaver.

Jude popped the pen cap between his rich lips, as if sucking on a lollipop, and released it. When he rounded the desk, his thick fingers glided across the top. He stopped in the middle, the fingers of his left hand still lingering on the desk's surface. He rested his buttocks against the edge while crossing his sturdy thighs.

His stance, a get-down-to-business sort of manner, should have intimidated Raven but failed. His brows-bunched-together stare and drawn-in cheeks seemed to coax her to lean in closer and rest her elbow on top of her own desk. She set her chin on her knuckles. "I'm completing them here tonight."

"Do you have any questions?"

She shook her head, still holding his stare. "I guess I should get comfy, huh?"

"Comfy?"

"Removed my toque and coat." She sat back, hands brushing the edge of her desk and arms spread wide.

About the Author

An Ojibway from Northwestern Ontario, Maggie resides in the country with her husband and their fur babies, two beautiful Alaskan Malamutes. When she's not writing, she can be found pulling weeds in the flower beds, mowing the huge lawn, walking the Mals deep in the bush, teeing up a ball at the golf course, fishing in the boat for walleye, or sitting on the deck at her sister's house, making more wonderful memories with the people she loves most.

Web Site: https://maggieblackbird.com/

Facebook Page: https://www.facebook.com/maggieblackbirdauthor/

Twitter: https://twitter.com/BlackbirdMaggie

BookbBub: https://www.bookbub.com/profile/maggie-blackbird

Linked In: https://www.linkedin.com/in/maggie-blackbird-032798169/

Newsletter Sign-Up: eepurl.com/gJu2VL

www.ingramcontent.com/pod-product-compliance
Lightning Source LLC
Chambersburg PA
CBHW070839120626
46556CB00002B/808

* 9 7 8 1 4 8 7 4 3 4 4 8 9 *